# The Chaucer Story Book

## By Eva March Tappan

### Illustrated

Sandycroft Publishing

The Chaucer Story Book

By Eva March Tappan

First published 1908

This edition ©2017

Sandycroft Publishing

http://sandycroftpublishing.com

ISBN 978-1542853040

# Contents

# Preface

IT has been somewhat the fashion of late to declare that the difficulty of reading Chaucer has been greatly overestimated. Probably it has—for some people. Chaucer, compared with Beowulf, for instance, is play. For one who knows a little French, a little German, and a little Latin, who has a shadowy recollection of Grimm's Law, a good memory for obsolete and half obsolete expressions, and a natural talent for discovering the gist of a word, no matter how it is spelled, it is a simple matter to read Chaucer. Doubtless, it would be better if everyone would read everything in the exact form which it took in its author's mind, *The Canterbury Tales* included; but, though most people claim to be able to appreciate humor, pathos, character-drawing, mischievous satire, and love of nature, and though all these qualities are found abundantly in the poetry of Chaucer, yet I have never met man, woman, or child who, without a preparation somewhat akin to that just outlined, had ever read *The Canterbury Tales* for pleasure. That is why *The Chaucer Story Book* has been written. The twelve stories chosen are those requiring fewest omissions to adapt them to the taste of the present day.

EVA MARCH TAPPAN.

*August 3, 1908.*

# I

# At the Tabard Inn

# At the Tabard Inn

HARRY BAILEY, landlord of the Tabard Inn, stood in the open doorway, listening. He heard the loud skirling of a bagpipe, the jingling of little bells, the slender notes of a flute, then a snatch of a song, and after it a hearty laugh. The tramping of hoofs sounded nearer and nearer, and up the street that led from London Bridge there came at an easy pace a company of riders.

"I'll warrant they're bound for the Tabard," said the landlord to himself; and he called to his serving men, "Ho there! Strew fresh rushes in the hall! Put another log on the fire! The air is cool when one has been riding. See you to it that the kitchen fire—"

There was no time for further orders, and no one could have heard them if they had been given, for the bagpipe was shrieking louder than ever, as if to show that great folk were close at hand; and in another moment the travelers were clattering into the yard of the inn, alighting from their horses, and climbing up the steps into the gallery and thence into the house.

What a company they were! It was no wonder that the grown folk as well as the children had stared at them curiously as they rode up the street. First of all came a tall, dignified knight, still wearing part of his armor and showing by the stains left on his *jupon,* or short tunic, that he had come directly from some campaign. His son followed him as squire, a handsome young man of twenty years

3

with curly hair and a merry face. No matter what the haste had been, *he* had found time to put on a fresh tunic, a beautiful one all embroidered with red and white flowers. It was he who had been playing so merrily on his flute as they rode up the street. Behind him came his yeoman, in hood and coat of green. He carried a bow and arrows, a sword and buckler, a horn, and a dagger. The pretty little nun, a prioress, who followed them, together with another nun and three priests, had taken time to make her toilet, too, for she looked as dainty and neat and smiling as if she had been riding through green fields instead of the dusty road. A rosary hung on her arm, with beads of gleaming coral gauded with green.

The little jingling bells were on the bridle rein of the most jovial of monks. His fiddle was in a bag at his side, his sleeves trimmed with the finest of fur, and his hood was fastened under his chin with a handsome clasp of good yellow gold, wrought into the shape of a love-knot. His horse was large and strong and richly caparisoned, and the monk rode as if he were as much at home on horseback as on his own feet.

"He rides like a hunter, and if I do not guess amiss, he would rather go a-hunting than sit in a cloister and pore over a book," thought a quiet traveler who was standing at a corner of the gallery, watching the newcomers with bright keen eyes. He had arrived at the inn that morning and on the following day he meant to ride on to Canterbury, for he was on a pilgrimage to the shrine of St. Thomas à Becket. His face was small and thoughtful, and he had a way of looking down upon the ground as if he were searching for something, or dreaming of something far away; but there was a gentle curve about his lips, as if he loved a jest and had a pretty wit of his own. He looked much amused when one of the company, a friar, laid aside his cowl so carefully. It was plain to see that it was well filled with knives and pins and other things to sell; and that he meant to do more than hear confessions and give absolutions,—he meant to make a penny or two for himself whenever he had a chance. He was humming a strain of a merry ballad, but he stopped as he came near a rather pompous-looking gentleman with a forked beard,—a merchant, for whom, or for whose money bags, the friar had evidently great respect. This merchant wore a tall Flemish hat with a long feather standing upright in it. The rest of his dress, too, was costly, and even the clasps of his shoes were of shining gold. No one could help seeing at a glance that he was a rich and prosperous man. He dismounted slowly and deliberately, as if he wanted everyone to understand that he was too great a personage to do anything in a hurry.

The merchant's handsome clothes made the slender young man who stood near him, waiting patiently for the way to be clear, look even shabbier than he would otherwise have done; and surely that was quite needless. His surtout was threadbare, his horse was thin as a rake, and the rider himself was not so very much stouter. "He's an Oxford student, a clerk, or I miss my guess," thought the watchful man on the gallery. "I'll warrant he'd rather have a score of books than all the costly robes the merchant ever brought across the Channel. He's a philosopher, but he does not seem to know how to turn base metal into gold."

After the Oxford student came two men who were talking quietly together, one a successful lawyer, wearing a cloak with a silken girdle all studded with little ornaments. The other was plainly a wealthy country gentleman. He had red cheeks and a long white beard. He carried a two-edged dagger, and a heavy silken purse hung at his side. Near these two stood a group of well-to-do folks—a haberdasher, a carpenter, a weaver, a dyer, and a draper. They were all dressed in the livery of their guild, and it was evidently one of wealth and importance. All that they wore was fresh and new and handsomely made. Even their knives were tipped with silver instead of brass. They had no idea of trusting to whatever sort of food they might find on the way, and they had wisely brought their cook along with them.

A brown-faced sea-captain had rolled himself off his steed rather awkwardly, for he was more accustomed to a ship than a horse. He wore a tunic of heavy frieze, and around his neck was a cord from which hung a dagger. "His beard has been shaken by many a tempest," thought the watcher on the gallery; and as he looked at the sailor's determined face, he said to himself, "I should not like to be among his prisoners. If I mistake not, he has made more than one man walk the plank."

All this while good Harry Bailey was going in and out among his guests, welcoming them to the inn. He bowed low before the doctor in his silk-lined gown; for a doctor, who knew the causes of all diseases, must be treated with respect. He jested gayly with a red-cheeked woman from Bath as he helped her to alight. Her hat was broad as a buckler. She wore scarlet stockings and bright new shoes.

"I'm an old traveler," she said. "I've been on pilgrimage before; I've been at Rome and Cologne, and three times at Jerusalem;" and she walked into the house with the air of one who had plenty of money and knew how to get the worth of it.

Two men were going up the steps side by side. They looked so much alike that it was plain they were brothers, though one wore the dress of a ploughman and the other that of a priest. Both had earnest faces, and the man on the gallery looked at them kindly, and said to himself, "There's a priest who will not run away from his country parish to find an easier place. I can fancy him taking his staff and setting out afoot in a storm to see a sick man."

Both of the brothers together did not take up so much room as the miller, who came after them in a blue hood and a long white coat. He was a stout, broad-shouldered fellow who would be sure of winning at a wrestling match. "I can break any door by running my head against it," he had boasted on the journey. His beard was as red as a fox, and when he opened his mouth, it looked like a great fiery furnace. Under his arm was a bagpipe, for it was he who had made all the skirling and shrieking as they were coming up the road. He was a very different man from the dignified knight, the kind-hearted priest, and the country gentleman with his pleasant, cheery face. So, too, was the summoner, whose business it was to call before the church court anyone whom he found breaking its laws. He looked so crafty and cruel that a child would have been afraid to come near him. A huge wreath was on his head and hung down over his red face. The man on the gallery smiled as he thought, "People always put out a bush when they have wine and beer." No sword or buckler had he, and it is hard to see how he could have managed a buckler, for he had all he could do to take care of a great round cake that he had brought with him. A pardoner rode beside him, his long, yellow hair hanging down upon his shoulders; for he fancied it the latest fashion to wear a cap, and so he had put his hood into the wallet which lay on the pommel of his saddle. The two men might well go together, for they were both cheats and got all the money they could from poor people who trusted them, or were in their power.

Last of all came the steward of an Inn of Court, and the reeve of a manor. Their faces were keen and shrewd, and one could see that they would make sharp bargains with whoever had dealings with them.

These were the people who had come to the Tabard Inn. They were all going on a pilgrimage to Canterbury; and, unlike as they were, they were glad of one another's company, for it was a journey of three or four days, and the larger the party the safer they were from robbers. Now there was bustle and tumult at the inn, serving men running here and there, and stable boys shouting to one another as they rubbed down the horses and put them into the stalls. The kitchen boys played tricks on the cooks, and the cooks scolded the kitchen boys; but it was not long before an agreeable fragrance began to fill the house, and soon the pilgrims were summoned to their supper. It was hardly more than the middle of the afternoon, but most people dined at ten in the morning, and the guests were ready for all the good things that their host had provided. The boards had been brought in and laid upon trestles. Then came the landlord, followed by serving men, each one with a towel around his neck and another on his left arm. After them came the kitchen boys with the various dishes. Bowls and napkins were passed around that the guests might wash their hands before the meal,—a somewhat desirable thing to do, as one wooden trencher generally served for two persons, and forks had not yet been invented.

The meats were cut into strips, and the guests dipped them into the sauce as they ate. The summoner devoured his meal greedily, and woe to the one who shared his trencher, for not a whit did he care if his whole fist went into the gravy. He swallowed garlic and onions by the handful, scattering lavish portions of his food over his unlucky neighbors. He gulped down the strongest wine and held out his cup again and again. Very different were the table manners of the prioress. Her little hand never went deep into the sauce, for at most she wet only the tips of her slender fingers. She knew how to carry a morsel from the trencher to her mouth without dropping the gravy; and before she drank, she always wiped her lips so carefully that never a bit of grease was left on the cup. She had listened well when tales were told of how people behaved at court, and she tried to practice the same manners. She had learned French, too, in her school days. She was delighted at the opportunity to use it, and never guessed that it was the French of Stratford-at-Bow rather than of Paris that she spoke.

Such a feast as it was for the hungry travelers! There were fish and fowl and meats of several kinds, lamb and pork served with ginger sauce, and roast beef served with garlic and vinegar; there was the flesh of the wild boar, generously seasoned with mustard; there were bacon and pea-soup, and the most amazing of puddings and pasties, manufactured of all sorts of remarkable articles mixed together and with many kinds of spice whose amount was limited only by their costliness. "Strong wine," or brandy, was poured upon these compounds, and then they were set afire and were brought in with flames shooting up to the low rafters. There was plenty of wine, served in goblets of wood and of pewter, and there was ale in abundance, for Southwark was famous for its ale.

Long before the supper was over, the early guest had made friends with the whole party. He had talked of warfare with the knight and of hunting with the monk. He had praised the singing of the friar and had made a neat little compliment to the pretty prioress. He had discussed with the merchant the danger of meeting pirates in the Channel, had asked the priest about the poor people of his parish, and had promised the loan of a book to the student; he had even jested with the summoner about his buckler of cake, and had playfully demanded of the miller whether he never took toll three times from the same bag of grain. Everyone was happy and good-natured. They washed their hands, paid their reckoning, and agreed to start early the next morning.

But now Harry Bailey had a word to say. He was tall and manly and fine-looking. During the supper he had sat in the seat of honor, by the pillar, and he had been the gayest of all. Now he said, "Sirs, you are heartily welcome, for you are certainly the merriest party that has been in this inn for a year. I'd like to do something to please you, and I have been thinking of a pastime that will amuse you and won't cost you a penny. You are going on a pilgrimage, and may God give you good speed; but there is no use in riding along as dumb as a stone. I know you mean to tell stories and enjoy yourselves. Now I have a plan, and if you do what I propose and are not the merrier for it, I'll give you my head." "What is it? Tell us what it is!" cried the pilgrims, and he replied, "This is it, that every one of you shall tell two stories going and two more on the homeward ride; and the one that tells the best story shall have a supper at the cost of the rest of us, and he shall sit in the place of honor, here by this post, when we have come back again. And to help carry out the sport; I will go with you at my own expense as guide, and if anyone opposes what I say, he shall pay every shilling that we spend on the road. If you like this, just say the word, and I will make myself ready.

Everybody was pleased and asked him to be their leader and the judge of the stories. A price was set for the supper, and the pilgrims all agreed to follow his decision in everything. Wine was brought, and they drank together in good fellowship. But now the sun was set, and everyone went to his rest.

# II

# The Knight's Tale

## PALAMON AND ARCITE

# The Knight's Tale

IN the morning, when day began to break, Harry Bailey awoke the pilgrims, and they all set out at a comfortable gait. When they had gone about two miles and had come to a place called the Watering of Saint Thomas, he stopped his horse and said, "Sirs, you remember what we planned last night. If you have not changed your minds, let us draw lots to see who shall tell the first story; and may I never again drink a cup of wine or of ale if the one that refuses does not have to pay all that we spend on the road. Now draw before we go any farther. The one that draws the shortest is to begin. Sir Knight," said he, "now draw your lot. Come my lady prioress. Mr. Clerk, don't be so modest; come forward, every man."

Each one drew, and whether it was by chance or whether the wily landlord had so arranged it, the fact is that the lot fell to the knight. Of course he would not break his agreement, and he said, "So I am to begin the game and tell the first story, am I? Let us ride on, then; and see to it that you listen well to every word."

So the pilgrims started up their horses, and the knight began his story. This is the tale that he told.

# PALAMON AND ARCITE

## I

ONCE upon a time there was a duke named Theseus who was lord of Athens. He was a great warrior, and one land after another had yielded to his sway. At length Scythia, too, fell into his hands; and there he found a wife as well as a kingdom, for he married Hippolita, the queen of the country. There was a great wedding, as you may imagine; and there was such pleasure at Athens that as the Duke and his beautiful bride drew near to the city walls, they could hear the shouts of rejoicing.

Just there the road made a turn, and behold, full in the way of the bridal procession was a company of ladies, all robed in somber black and kneeling two by two. Not a word did they say, but they wept and wailed and caught hold of the Duke's bridle rein with such lamenting as was never heard in the world before.

"Who are you that disturb my feast with your crying? Are you so envious of my happiness? Speak out, and if anyone has done you a wrong, tell me what I shall do to avenge you." So said the Duke.

Then spoke the oldest of the ladies, her face as white as death. "Have mercy upon us," she pleaded. "Pity us and help us. For fourteen long days we have awaited your coming to beg for your aid; for we are naught but beggars now, though once every one of us was either a queen or a duchess."

Then Duke Theseus and the Queen Hippolita and the men-at-arms and all the long procession stopped and listened to the sorrowful tale of the ladies in black. It seemed that at the siege of Thebes their husbands had all been slain, and Creon, lord of Thebes, had declared that the bodies should be given to the dogs and should receive none of the honors of burial.

Duke Theseus was so sorry for the poor ladies that he felt as if his own heart would break. He leaped down from his horse and raised them from the dust, and comforted them as best he could. "I swear to you," he said, "as I am a faithful knight, that your wrongs shall be avenged. Not one half day will I tarry even to celebrate my wedding; and before long it shall be told from end to end of Greece how Theseus put to death the wicked Creon. Do you keep watch and ward over my bride," he bade his chamberlains, "and lead her safely into Athens." There was not time for another word; the Duke had already flung out his great white war banner, whereon was a blood-red figure of Mars with glittering spear and shield. Beside the banner waved a pennon of richest gold, into which was beaten the image of the Minotaur that once he slew in Crete.

So it was that Duke Theseus and the noblest of his army rode onto the walls of Thebes and called the king forth to battle. The Duke slew the wicked Creon and put his men to flight. He even took the city by assault and tore down the wall, beam and rafter. To the mourning women he gave the bodies of their husbands, that the rites of burial might be bestowed. Then he pitched his tent on the battlefield for the night and made himself ready to return on the following morning to Athens and his bride Hippolita.

All that night the pillagers did their work on the field of battle, and stripped the dead bodies of mail, weapons, and garments. And it chanced that, lying in a heap of the slain, they came upon two young knights on whose tabards the same device was richly embroidered. By this device the heralds knew well that the young men were the sons of two sisters of the blood royal of Thebes. "It may be that the Duke will take ransom for them," thought the pillagers, and they carried them gently to the tent of Theseus, for the life was not yet fully gone from them. Theseus would accept no ransom. He sent the two knights straightway to Athens to be flung into prison. Then he and his army rode homeward, and he wore a crown of laurel as a victor. In his castle he dwelt in joy and honor; but closely guarded in a tower of stone abode Palamon and Arcite, for those were the names of the two young men, and they dwelt in suffering and misery.

Now when Hippolita came to Athens, she brought in her train her young sister Emily, who was fairer than the lily upon its stalk of green and fresher than the Maytime with its new-blown flowers, for truly her bloom was like that of the rose. It came to pass one bright May morning that she arose from her sleep and went out into the garden. Her dress was dainty and pretty, and adown her back fell her braid of golden hair a full yard long. Up and down the paths she strolled, picking here and there a flower of white or red to make herself a wreath. She was singing softly; and, truly, her voice was like that of an angel.

Now the dungeon tower of the castle rose hard by the garden wall, and Palamon was pacing to and fro in a chamber high up from the ground. There was a little window, closely grated with heavy bars of iron, and through it he could see the city, or, if he looked downward, the castle garden. As the Fates would have it, he caught a glimpse of Emily. Thereupon he turned pale and cried "Ah!" as if he were pierced to the heart. At that Arcite started up and called, "Cousin, cousin, what troubles you? You are white as death. Why did you cry out? For God's sake, be patient, for we can do naught else. Our evil stars have given us this fate and we must endure it."

"O cousin," replied Palamon, "it was not of our prison that I cried out, but because of the beautiful maiden in the garden down below. The love of her has pierced my heart, and it will surely be my death. I know not whether she be woman or goddess. Perchance it is Venus herself." And down upon his knees he fell, and prayed aloud, "O Venus, if it be indeed yourself, help us out of this dungeon. Have pity upon us!"

Then Arcite looked through the iron-barred window and caught a glimpse of the maiden; and he, too, was grievously wounded by her beauty. "Alas," he moaned, "if I may not have her favor, if I may not at the least see her close at hand, I shall surely die."

"What?" demanded Palamon. "Do you say this in jest or in earnest?"

"In earnest," replied Arcite. "May God help me. I am in no mood for jesting."

Then Palamon knit his brows angrily. "I am your cousin and your brother-in-arms," said he; "and we have sworn solemnly never to hinder each other in love or in any other case, but to help each other as most we may. And now, like a false traitor, you dare to love my lady whom I shall love and serve so long as my heart shall beat. I loved her first and told my love to you, and you are in honor bound to help me, or else you are but a false traitor and a treacherous knight."

"You are more likely to prove a false knight than I," Arcite replied proudly, "and, indeed, you are already false. You do not know even now whether she is a woman or a goddess. You love her as one might love a saint, but I love her as a woman, and I told you so as my sworn brother. Even if you had loved her first, don't you know the old saying, 'Who shall give law to a lover?' A man cannot help his love if he die for it. But, my brother, we are prisoners for life; no ransom will set us free. There is small chance that the fair maiden will ever look with favor upon either of us. Love her if you will; but so shall I, and that is the end of it, dear brother. We must stay here in prison, and each of us must bear his fate."

Now it came to pass that a certain noble duke named Perotheus, a childhood's friend of Theseus, came to Athens to visit him; they had known each other in Thebes for many a year, and loved each other most tenderly. Duke Perotheus begged for his freedom, and finally, to give his friend a pleasure, Duke Theseus set the prisoner free. "But beware," he charged "for if ever you are found in any part of my realm, you will lose your head by the sword."

Then was Arcite free, and he went to his own home; but he wept and wailed and groaned and aloud and even sought to take his life. "Alas, that ever I knew Perotheus!" he lamented. "But for him I might have dwelt forever in the prison of Theseus. How blissful should I have been to see her whom I love and serve, even though I might never win her favor. O dear cousin Palamon," he groaned, "the victory is yours. You are in prison, indeed, but it is a paradise, for you may sometimes cast your eyes upon my lady. You are a knight, worthy and skillful, and by some change of fortune you may someday win your heart's desire; but neither earth, air, fire, water, nor any creature made of them can help me or give me comfort. Alas, we know not what we pray for. I thought that if I could only get out of prison, I should be happy indeed; but since I cannot see you, Emily, I might as well be dead."

On the other hand, Palamon, when he knew that Arcite was gone, made the tower echo with his groans and cries. "O my cousin Arcite," he wailed, "little do you care now for my suffering. You are free and in our own Thebes. It will be easy for you to get our kinsfolk together and make so fierce a war upon this town that by treaty you may have Emily for your wife, while I weep and wail here in this prison tower, and my heart is pierced unto death with the love of her."

["Now tell me," said the knight, "all you who be lovers, which one was in the worse case, Palamon or Arcite? Palamon could see his lady every day, but he could never be free from his prison. Arcite was at liberty to wander whither he would, but never again could he set his eyes upon the love of his heart."]

17

# II

Now when Arcite had come to Thebes, he sighed, and groaned full many a day and thought no one ever had such trouble as he. He grew pale and thin, his eyes were hollow, he cared naught for meat or drink, and when the time for sleep had come, he lay on his bed and moaned and groaned all the night long. After a year or two of this suffering, he dreamed one night that the god Mercury stood before him and said, "Cheer up, Arcite. You are soon to journey to Athens, and there your woe shall have an end."

Then Arcite started up from his sleep. "Whatever comes," he declared, "I will go to Athens. Life or death, I will see my lady." He caught sight of his face in a mirror, and it was so changed that he said to himself, "If I but take some lowly place, I can live in Athens all my life unknown, and see my lady every day." Straightway he dressed himself as a poor laborer, and with a squire in like disguise he went to Athens the next morning, and to the very gate of the palace. Fortune favored him, for when the chamberlain of the fair Emily saw the young man at the gate so stout and big of bone, he hired him at once to hew wood for the fires and to carry water.

For a year or two, Philostrate, as he now called himself, did the work of a servant; but he was so courteous and so kindly that the whole court loved him and begged Duke Theseus to put him in some higher position. So Theseus made him squire of his chamber, and gave him gold to maintain his rank, never guessing that each year the squire's revenue from his own estates was brought him privily. For three years Arcite lived in this happiness, and so won the heart of the Duke that there was no man dearer to him.

All these seven years poor Palamon was pining away in his prison, but in the seventh year, on the third night of May, it came about that by the help of a good friend he got free. He fled as fast as ever he could to a grove where he meant to hide all day, and then, when the night had come, to make his way to Thebes. There he intended to beg his friends to help him make war upon Athens; and thus he would either lose his life or win Emily as his bride.

Now the busy lark, day's messenger, was greeting the gray dawning with her song, the fiery sun was rising, and all the east was laughing with the light, and the warm beams were drying in the groves the silver drops that hung upon the leaves. It chanced that on that very morning Arcite arose early and rode out to the fields to pay his homage to the month of May. He galloped onward a mile or two, and then, as Fortune would have it, he rode into the very grove where Palamon was hidden. He was in search of hawthorn leaves for a wreath; and as he rode, he sang for joy,—

> "Welcome, welcome, lovely May,
> Trees and flowers are fresh and gay;
> Grant me hawthorn leaves, I pray."

After he had roamed about as he would and had sung all his merry roundelay, he suddenly turned grave, as lovers are wont to do; for in their moods they are first up, then down, like a bucket in a well. He sat him down under a tree and sighed. "Alas," he said, "for the day that I was born. Here am I of the blood royal of Thebes, and I serve my mortal enemy humbly as his squire. I dare not avow my own name. I am no longer Arcite, but Philostrate. O cruel Mars and Juno, it is you who have destroyed all our race save wretched me and Palamon, whom Theseus keeps in prison. And besides all this, my heart is pierced through and through with the fiery darts of love. Emily, Emily, it is for you that I am dying;" and down he fell in a trance.

Palamon had heard every word, and he felt as if a sword had been run through his heart. He shook with anger, and with face deadly pale he started out from the thick bushes and cried, "Arcite, false and wicked traitor as you are that you dare to love my lady for whom I bear all this woe, you are of my blood and have sworn to be true to me. You have cheated Duke Theseus, and you bear a false name. I am Palamon, your deadly enemy; and now, even though I am barely from prison, and though I have no kind of weapon, yet one or the other of us shall die, for you shall not love my lady Emily."

Arcite drew his sword, fierce as a lion. "If you had a weapon and if you were not beside yourself with love, you should never leave this place alive," he said. "Love is free, and I will love her in spite of all that you can do. Tonight I will bring you meat and drink and bed, and tomorrow I will come here secretly with two suits of armor. You shall choose the better and I will take the worse. Then if it should chance that you are victor, you may have your lady for all me;" and so they parted for the night.

It came to pass as Arcite had said, and in the morning, without any word of salutation, each helped the other to arm; and then they fought with their sharp spears as savagely as if Palamon were a lion and Arcite a tiger; and soon they were up to their ankles in blood.

Now Duke Theseus was a famous hunter, and as luck would have it, he set forth this very morning in pursuit of a great deer that he had heard was in this grove. With him rode his Queen Hippolita and her fair sister Emily, dressed all in hunter's green. Behold, when they came to the grove, there were Palamon and Arcite fighting as fiercely as two wild boars. The Duke spurred on his courser, and in a moment he stood between them. "Stop!" he cried, and drew his sword. "Who strikes another blow shall die. Who are you that dare to fight here as if you were in the royal lists?"

Then said Palamon, "What need is there of words? We both deserve death, and we both are weary of our lives. Slay me and slay my fellow as well; for know that he is Arcite, your mortal enemy, who is banished from your realm on pain of death. He called his name Philostrate, and for many a year he has deceived you; because he loved Emily and could not live away from her. I am the wretched Palamon. I have broken out of your prison, and I, as well as he, am your mortal foe. I, too, love the fair Emily, and so fervently that I would die in her sight."

The Duke responded, "Your own mouth has condemned you, and you shall surely die."

At this the Queen and Emily and all the ladies of their company began to weep. They fell down at the feet of the Duke and begged for mercy upon the prisoners, whose only fault was their love. At first the Duke had been exceedingly angry, but pity rises soon in a noble heart, and he said to the cousins, "At the request of the Queen and my dear sister Emily I forgive you; but you must swear never to do harm to my country, but to be my friends and help me in every way that you can." The knights took a solemn oath that they would be true to him, and then he continued, "So far as lineage goes, either of you might wed a princess or a queen; but you know well enough that even if you should fight forever, Emily could not marry both of you. Now go freely where you will, and fifty weeks from today return, each with one hundred knights, armed and ready to fight. I give you my word as a knight that he whom fortune favors shall have Emily for his wife."

Down upon their knees fell Palamon and Arcite and every other person present, and thanked the Duke with all their hearts. Then joyfully the two young men set out for their home city of Thebes.

## III

WHEN the appointed day had come, the cousins appeared in Athens, each with his hundred knights well armed for battle. Never was there so noble a company before, for every man who would win honor for his name had pleaded to be one of the number. Each one was armed to suit himself. Some wore coats of mail, some breastplates and short tunics; some wore plate armor, and some carried Prussian shields. Some were well guarded on their legs and carried axes, and others bore war-maces of steel. With Palamon came Lycurgus, King of Thrace, a tall, broad-shouldered man with heavy black beard. Under his shaggy eyebrows he glared about him like an angry hawk. His long hair, black as a raven's wing, hung down his back, and a massive wreath of gold rested on his head, sparkling with rubies and diamonds. Over his shoulders a coal-black bearskin was thrown. He did not ride on horseback, but, according to the custom of his country, in a golden chariot drawn by four white bulls. A score or more of white boar hounds as big as steers leaped about him, and in his train there came one hundred lords with brave, fierce hearts.

With Arcite was the renowned Emetreus, king of India. He rode upon a bay horse with steel trappings and a covering of cloth of gold. His tabard was of silk, thickly embroidered with great white pearls. His saddle was of burnished gold. Over his shoulders was no rough bearskin, but a mantle embroidered with sparkling rubies. His curly hair was as golden as the sunshine. His nose was high, his eyes were bright, his lips were full, and his color fresh, and if Lycurgus looked about him like a hawk, Emetreus's glare was like that of a lion, and his voice was like a trumpet. On his head he wore a wreath of laurel, and on his wrist he carried a tame eagle white as a lily. Tame lions and leopards ran about him as he rode. With him were one hundred lords in all their armor save their helmets. They were richly dressed, for in this company were dukes and earls and even kings. So it was that early Sunday morning the rival parties came up to the city. Duke Theseus led them within the walls and made a bounteous feast to do them honor, with viands rich and gifts to great and small and noble minstrelsy.

On Monday morning, two hours before the dawn, Palamon went to the temple of Venus and prayed for her help. Naught cared he for glory or the renown of victory he said; all he asked was to have Emily for his wife; and if he could not have her, he begged that he might die in the contest. The statue of Venus trembled and made a sign to him. "My prayer is granted," he cried, and went home joyfully.

Three hours after Palamon had gone to the temple, Emily, too, set out to offer sacrifice and ask for the favor of Diana. She and her maidens went to the temple of the goddess, bearing with them incense, handsome robes, horns of mead, and coals of fire. Emily's golden hair was all unbound, and on her head lay a wreath of green oak leaves. She kindled two fires upon the altar, and thus she prayed to pure Diana, "O goddess, thou dost know well that I would ever have my freedom and die like thee unwed. I pray thee that the ardent love of Palamon and Arcite may be turned from me to some other maiden; or, if my fate decrees that I must become the wife of one of the two, grant that I may fall to him who loves me most." Then there came to pass a marvel indeed, for one of the fires went out, then blazed again; and straightway the other fire, too, went out; but as it paled and died away, there was a strange whistling sound like that which a wet log makes when it is laid upon a fire, and at the end of the firebrand there trickled out full many a drop of blood of scarlet-red. It was small wonder that Emily wept with fear, for who could tell what this might portend? Then there came to pass an even greater marvel, for before the terrified maiden stood the goddess herself, dressed as a huntress and bearing bow and quiver. She spoke to Emily gently and said, "My daughter, do not grieve. It is decreed of the gods that you shall become the bride of one of those two who for your sake have borne such suffering; but to which of them the Fates forbid that I should disclose. Read well my altar, for the fires will reveal your fate;" and in a moment she was gone. "The fires will reveal your fate," Emily said over and over to herself, but what the prediction meant she could not understand. "O kind goddess," she cried, "I give myself to you. I put myself under your care and protection;" and then she left the temple and went quickly to her home.

Arcite, too, sought the favor of the gods, and at the fourth hour of the morning he went to the temple of Mars to make sacrifice to the god of war; and thus he prayed, "O powerful god, in every land the fate of battle is determined by thy word. I beg thee to look kindly upon my sacrifice. Pity my suffering, and think upon the days when thou, too, didst burn with love for Venus and didst grieve and sorrow when not to thee but to Vulcan she was given. I am young, as thou wast then, and I have experienced little of life, and yet I know right well that my suffering is greater than men ever endured before, for she who has so pierced my heart cares not whether I live or die. By force of arms I must win her ere she will show me favor. Help me in my battle on the morrow, and the glory of the victory shall be thine. I promise to hang up my banner and my arms in thy temple and to do it reverence so long as I shall live. My beard and hair, which never yet have felt the touch of razor or of shears, I will sacrifice to thee, and I will be thy true and faithful servant to the last day of my life." To Arcite, too, was shown a marvel. The doors of the temple shook, the fires blazed up so bright on the altar that the whole building was aglow, and the ground gave out a fragrant smell. Arcite stood still in wonder. Then he cast more incense upon the fire. And as he gazed, he heard a gentle ringing come from the god's coat of mail, and a low voice that murmured, "Victory;" and Arcite went back to his inn as happy as a bird in the sunshine.

Now there was trouble on Olympus, for Venus had agreed to help Palamon, and Mars had promised the victory to Arcite. Jupiter was at his wit's end, and at last he called upon Saturn and asked that from his long experience he would devise some way to bring about peace. Then said Saturn to Venus, "Weep no more, my child. Thy Palamon shall have his lady as thou hast promised; and yet in due time there shall be harmony again between you and Mars."

## IV

ALL that Monday there was feasting and jousting and dancing; but on Tuesday at the dawn of day there was heard from every inn the stamping of horses, the clashing of arms, and then the tramping of hoofs, as party after party of lords on steeds and palfreys rode up to the palace gates. The suits of mail were quaint and rich with finest work of steel, embroidery, and goldsmithing. Bright were shields and testers and trappings, helmets of beaten gold, and hauberks. Lords sat upon their coursers in gorgeous array, knights formed in long lines of retinue, squires were busy nailing heads upon spears, buckling helmets, fitting straps to shields, and lacing armor with leathern thongs; no one was idle. The foaming steeds champed their golden bits, the armorers ran to and fro with files and hammers. There were yeomen on foot and crowds of the common sort with their short staves. There were pipes and trumpets and drums and clarions. The palace was full of people roaming about or gathered in little groups to discuss the champions. "That man with the black beard will win," said one. "No, rather he with the bald head," declared another. One stood by a certain knight because he had a grim and savage look, and another upheld his favorite because his battle-axe weighed full twenty pounds.

Duke Theseus did not leave his chamber till both the Theban knights had come to the palace. Then he seated himself at a window in most handsome array. The crowds pressed closer and closer about him. Near at hand was a high platform, and on this stood a herald. "Ho! Ho!" he cried; and when the people had become quiet, he told them the will of the Duke.

"Our gracious lord hath considered in his wisdom that it is a foolish waste of noble blood to fight this tournament as if it were a mortal battle. This, then, is what he decrees: On pain of death let no man bring to the lists any kind of dart or pole-axe or short knife or short sword with biting point. No one shall ride more than one course against his fellow with a sharp-ground spear; though he may defend himself on foot if he will. He that is overcome shall not be slain, but brought to the stake that shall be set on either side; and there he shall remain. And if it chance that the leader on either side be captured or slay his adversary, then shall the tourney come straightway to an end. God speed you. Go forth to the contest. Fight your fill with long sword and with battle hammer. Now go your way. This is our lord's decree."

The people shouted till the heavens rang. "God bless our gentle lord," they cried, "who forbids the useless shedding of blood." The trumpets sounded, and up through the streets all draped with cloth of gold rode the brilliant troop. First came the noble Duke Theseus with Palamon on his right and Arcite on his left, and after them rode the queen and her sweet sister Emily. Then followed the long, rich procession; and before it was fully nine in the morning, they were at the lists. Never were there such lists in the world before. The ground was a mile about. There were walls of stone, and beyond them a moat. Seats rose above seats to the height of sixty paces. To the east there was a gate of white marble, and to the west there was its fellow. It might well be a splendid theater, for whenever Duke Theseus had heard of a man who was skilled in building or in carving, he had offered him food and goodly wages if he would come to him and do his best. That pious rites and sacrifices might be paid to the gods, an oratory with an altar was built above the eastern gate in honor of Venus; and above the western gate stood another in honor of Mars. To the north, in a turret on the wall, was a third oratory, rich with white alabaster and red coral. These were the temples to which the two young knights and Emily had resorted to make their respective appeals. Such was the place where the tournament was to be held.

Now when Duke Theseus and the Queen Hippolita and the fair Emily and the ladies-in-waiting were seated and the whole company had found places, then through the western gateway, under the chapel of Mars, came Arcite and the hundred men of his party with a banner of scarlet-red. At the same instant Palamon passed with his followers through the eastern gate under the chapel of Venus. His banner gleamed white and his face was brave and hardy. Never were there two such companies, for the wisest man in the world could not have seen that either was less worthy than the other in wealth or age or bearing. They drew up opposite each other in two fair lines. The herald read the names from his list that everyone might see that there was no treachery or deceit. Then the two gates were closed, and he cried in a loud voice, "Do your devoir, you proud young knights!"

The trumpets and the clarions reechoed. The spears on either side went firmly into rest, and the sharp spurs pierced the flanks of the horses. The arrows splintered on the heavy shields; one felt a sharp stab go through his breast; spears sprang up twenty feet on high; swords flashed out like silver; helmets were split and shattered; blood burst out in fierce red streams; bones were crushed by the mighty blows of the battle hammers. The war horse stumbled and fell, and his rider rolled under his feet like a ball. One man thrust with the butt of his broken spear, and another on horseback trampled him down. One was so badly hurt that he was taken prisoner and brought to the stake; another was dragged to the stake on the opposing side. And then Duke Theseus bade them rest and drink if so they would.

Many a time had the two cousins met. Each of them had unhorsed the other twice. No tiger whose whelp had been stolen was ever so savage as Arcite; no lion was ever so mad with hunger for the blood of his prey as was Palamon for Arcite's life. The strokes fell heavy upon their helmets, and the red blood flowed from both.

All things, however, have an end. Before the sun had come to its setting, while Palamon was fighting fiercely with Arcite, King Emetreus struck him a terrible blow with the sword. Palamon, striving with Arcite as he was, turned upon his foe and bore him a sword's length out of his saddle. It was all in vain, and Palamon, struggling against them every step of the way, was seized, and by the strength of twenty was dragged to the stake. King Lycurgus had gone to his rescue, and he, too, was struck down.

Then, indeed, was Palamon in sorrow, for not another blow might he strike. And as soon as Duke Theseus saw what had happened, he cried, "Hold! The fight is done, and Emily belongs to Arcite of Thebes." Then arose such shouts of rejoicing that it seemed as if the very walls would crumble.

Venus, up above, wept till her tears dropped down into the lists, and cried, "Verily, I am disgraced forever; but Saturn replied, "Peace, daughter, peace. Mars has his wish, his knight has all that he asked; and soon you, too, shall have your will."

And now while the heralds were shouting and the trumpets blowing and the people crying aloud for joy, behold, a wonder came to pass. Arcite had doffed his helmet and was galloping along the lists. He looked up to his Emily, and in return she gave him a friendly glance; but Saturn had gone for aid to Pluto, king of the lower world, and from the ground, full in the face of Arcite's steed, there flashed out a flame of the infernal fire. The frightened charger leaped aside, foundered, and flung his rider upon the hard earth, his breast crushed with the saddlebow and bleeding sorely. Sadly they lifted him up and carried him to the palace. They freed him tenderly from his armor and laid him in a bed; and all the while he called for Emily.

Duke Theseus came home with all his retinue. There was great rejoicing, for it was said not only that Arcite would not die, but, strange to tell, that not one man of the whole company had been slain. To be sure, the breastbone of one had been pierced with a spear, and there was many a broken bone and many a wound; but some had salves, and some had charms, or drinks of healing herbs. All that night there was revelry and feasting in honor of the stranger lords. The noble Duke did his best to honor every man and give him comfort; though, truth to tell, small comfort was needed, for there is no disgrace in making a slip or falling nor is it a shame for one man to be dragged to the stake by the might of twenty.

That there should be no envy or jealousy between the two parties, the good Duke Theseus had the fame of both sides cried abroad. For three full days he entertained the whole company with royal feasting; and when the time came for them to go to their homes, he gave them noble escort a long day's journey on their way.

But now it came to pass that the wound of Arcite would not heal, and soon it was spread through the city that he must die. When Arcite knew this, he sent for Emily and also for Palamon. "O my lady, whom I most dearly love!" he said, "alas for the pains that I have borne for you! Queen of my heart, farewell. For the love of God, raise me gently in your arms and listen well to what I would say. For love of you I have had strife and anger with my cousin; but now I tell you frankly that in all this world there is no other man so worthy of your love as Palamon." Hardly had he thus spoken before the chill of death came over him, his sight grew dim, and his breath began to fail; but still he kept his eyes upon his lady, and his last word was "Emily."

Then Palamon cried out with grief, and Emily wept both night and day; and in the town young and old grieved for the death of Arcite. No man sorrowed more than Theseus; and the good Duke sought how he could pay most of honor and respect to his friend. At last he concluded that the funeral pyre should be built in that same grove where the cousins had fought their fight for love. He sent for a bier and draped it all with cloth of gold, the richest that he had. With cloth of gold he robed Arcite. White gloves were drawn upon the dead knight's hands, and upon his head was laid a laurel crown, while in his right hand was placed a sword of keen, bright edge. The Duke gazed upon the face of his friend and wept so that it was sad to hear him. Then, that the people might one and all look upon the knight whom they loved, the Duke had the body carried to the hall, and that soon reechoed with their cries of mourning.

Hither came Palamon with unkempt beard and hair rough with ashes. His clothes were black and well bedewed with tears. Hither, too, came Emily, the saddest of the company. Then Duke Theseus bade three noble white steeds be led forth all trapped with glittering steel and distinguished by the arms of Arcite. On the first steed sat a rider who bore the dead man's shield; on the second was one who held his spear; and on the third a man who carried his Turkish bow with its case of beaten gold. The noblest of the Greeks took up the bier, and then, their eyes red with tears, they passed slowly through the main street of the city, where all was draped with mourning. On the left walked Duke Theseus, and on the right his aged father Egeus, carrying in their hands golden vessels well filled with honey and blood and milk and wine. After them came Palamon with a noble train, and sorrowing Emily, bearing a brand of fire.

In the grove a mighty pyre had been reared. First, many loads of straw were spread upon the ground. Upon that was laid dry wood well split, then green wood of fir and birch and elm and ash and oak and many other kinds. Spices rich and rare were sprinkled upon the heap, and it was draped with cloth of gold and jeweled broidery. Garlands were hung upon it bright with flowers, and over it all handfuls of myrrh and sweet-smelling incense were cast. So lofty was the pyre that the green branches reached upward to the skies; and so broad was it that it stretched out full twenty fathoms.

When the sorrowing company had come to the little grove, then Emily herself must kindle the funeral fire, for such was the custom of the land. She touched the dry wood with the torch; the fire blazed up, and at the sight she fell fainting to the ground. As the fire burned, men threw into it their jewels, their raiment, their spears and shields, with cups of wine and milk and blood. Three times the Greeks rode all about the pyre with piercing cries; three times with clashing spears; three times the women called aloud. When the pyre had burned to ashes, they went sadly back to the city, and Palamon returned to Thebes.

Now after several years had passed, Athens planned to form an alliance with certain countries. A parliament was to be held in that city, and Duke Theseus asked Palamon to be present. Sorrowful and still in mourning garments, Palamon bowed before the Duke and stood in silence, waiting to learn his will. Then Theseus sent for Emily, and when the place was hushed, he spoke. "The Creator of this world has decreed," he said, "that all things shall have an end. The oak lives long, but at the last it falls. Even the stone on which we tread wastes away as it lies by the roadside. Everyone must die, page and king alike. Therefore ought we to make a virtue of necessity and not rebel against Him who guides the course of all. Now without doubt a man is most sure of honorable fame who dies in the very flower of his excellence, and his truest friends should rejoice at his death in the midst of his honors rather than when old age has made his deeds forgotten and his service is no longer remembered. Why do we longer mourn that our beloved Arcite has left this life in the glory of his knighthood? Why do his cousin and his bride, who loved him so well, murmur at his well-being? They only fret his soul and their own hearts. Therefore I urge that we no longer grieve, but that, even before we leave this place, we make of two sorrows one perfect joy to last forevermore. Sister," said he, "this is my edict, given forth with full agreement of my councilors, that noble Palamon, your own true knight, who loves you with all his heart and has so done since the first day that he saw your face, shall feel your tender mercy and shall become your lord and husband. Give me your hand in token of your womanly pity."

Then said he to Palamon, "I believe that little arguing is needed to win your assent to this. Come near and take your lady by the hand."

So came it to pass that with all joy and song Palamon became the husband of his chosen lady. Emily loved him so tenderly, and he served her so devotedly, that never was there a word of jealousy or any other trouble between them; and to the end of their days they lived in health and wealth and happiness.

# III

# The Man of Law's Tale

## THE STORY OF CONSTANCE

# The Man of Law's Tale

WHEN the knight had ended his tale, everyone in the company, old or young, declared that it was a noble story. Harry Bailey cried heartily, "That's going well. The budget is open, and now let us see who will tell the next. Sir man of law," he went on, "you agreed to obey my commands; now keep your promise."

"Surely," replied the lawyer. "I have no thought of breaking my agreement. A promise is a debt, and I would ever keep my word. The laws that we make for others, we must ourselves obey;" and without delay he began this tale.

## THE STORY OF CONSTANCE

IN Syria there once lived a company of merchants who were so successful that their spices and satins and cloth of gold were sent far and wide. In the course of their business it came about that they spent some time in Rome. When they returned to Syria, the Sultan sent for them, as was his custom when they had been journeying to foreign parts, that he might learn about other kingdoms and hear of whatever wonders they had seen.

The merchants told him much about Rome, of the greatness of the buildings and the magnificence of the Emperor; but the beginning and end of every story was Lady Constance, the Emperor's fair daughter. "Never was there such a maiden since the world began," they said. "She is the most beautiful woman in the world, and yet she has no touch of pride. She is young, but, indeed, she has no foolish childishness. She is kind and charitable. She is the embodiment of courtesy, and her heart is the very chamber of purity."

The merchants returned to their homes, but their words did not fade from the memory of the Sultan. By day and by night he thought of the beautiful maiden, and at length he sent for his privy council and charged them upon their fealty to get him Constance for his wife. The privy councilors were at their wits' end. "It is some evil magic," they whispered to one another; but to the Sultan they said, "Sir, we are the faithful servants of our blessed prophet Mahomet; and we do greatly fear that no Christian ruler would give his daughter in marriage to one who obeys the prophet's laws."

But all the Sultan would reply was, "I will be christened rather than lose her. Keep your fears to yourselves and get me Constance."

Then there was much journeying to and fro. Ambassadors were sent to the Emperor and to the Pope and to men of mark either in the church or in knighthood; and ambassadors were sent from them to Syria. The Sultan agreed to become a Christian if he might have Constance; and finally, after much debate and discussion, it was decided that for the advantage of the true faith the Emperor's daughter should become the Sultan's wife. Then throughout Rome went the Emperor's command that every person in the town should pray most earnestly for a blessing upon the journey and the marriage.

Constance wept sorely that she must go far away from her home and friends to live among a barbarous people and become the wife of one whom she knew not; but the decree was passed. She said meekly, "Christ give me grace to obey his will," and she set to work in heaviness of heart to make ready for the marriage. When the day had come to take ship, she bade farewell to all and went on board; and with her went a long train of lords and ladies and knights and bishops and also a great weight of gold to be her dowry.

Now the wicked mother of the Sultan had done everything in her power to oppose the will of her son. When she saw that this was of no use, she planned to bring about by trickery what she could not accomplish by honest means. One night she secretly called her own councilors together, and when they had come, she took her seat and thus she spoke: "My lords, you all know that my son is about to prove false to the laws which God gave by his blessed apostle Mahomet; but as for me, I will tear the life from my body rather than the Koran from my heart. If you will follow my advice, I promise you that we shall dwell safely on earth to our days' end, and after that shall realize all the joys of heaven." Each one took a solemn oath that he would stand by her and would persuade as many of his friends as possible to do the same; and then she revealed her cruel plot. "First, we will let them baptize us as Christians—cold water will not hurt us—and after that I will give a feast; and the Sultan's wife shall be made so red that it will need a whole font of water to wash her white."

As the evil woman had planned, so it came to pass. She went to the palace of the Sultan and said with feigned sorrow, "My son, I grieve deeply that I have been a heathen so long a time. I will no longer believe in Mahomet, and I am ready to be baptized by a Christian priest. And grant," she pleaded, "that I may make a feast for the Christian folk. If they will but come to me, I will do my best to please them." The Sultan was so rejoiced that he hardly knew what to say. He fell upon his knees before her and with great joy he thanked her most heartily.

Now when the Christian folk had come to land, the whole Syrian kingdom turned out to meet them. There were vast crowds of Syrians and of Romans, all dressed in their richest array, but most brilliantly attired of all was the mother of the Sultan; and certainly no daughter could have been greeted more tenderly than was the gentle Constance by this enemy who plotted night and day for her ruin. And as for the Sultan himself, no words can tell the joy with which he welcomed his beautiful young bride.

After a little, the time was at hand when the Christians should be entertained by the mother of the Sultan. Truly, she had kept her word, for the tables were loaded with dainties from every part of the kingdom and from many a realm that was far away from the land of Syria. But suddenly the signal was given, and almost in a moment the Sultan and all the Christians at the board were struck down dead save Constance alone. The Sultaness, for by this murder of her son the wicked woman had made herself ruler of the kingdom, on that same day flung the helpless Constance into a rudderless vessel and thrust it out upon the sea. "Get to Italy as best you can," she cried pitilessly. The dowry that Constance had brought with her was put on board the ship, and by someone's kindness a store of clothes and of food was added.

When Constance found herself alone on the deep sea, she knelt down and upon her breast she made the sign of the cross, and piteously she begged, "O holy Christ, be with me, and when the day comes that the stormy waters shall swallow me, keep me, I pray, from the powers of evil, and bring me unto thy everlasting bliss."

Day after day went by until three years and more had passed. He who had saved her from the slaughter at the feast cared for her now, and kept her from all harm. The ship drifted on and on, far beyond the seas of Greece, and at length it floated through the strait that lies between the Moorish country and the land of Spain and out into the wide, wide ocean. One morning it came close to far Northumberland, and rising from the shore Constance saw a castle. A storm wind drove the ship upon a sandbar, and so fast was it that even the coming of the tide had no power to set it free. The constable of the castle saw the wreck, and he went down to the shore. There was the broken ship all beaten by the waves, and on its deck stood the weary, lonely woman, and with her the great treasure that had been her dowry. She begged for pity, and the good constable brought her tenderly to the shore. And when her feet first touched the land, she kneeled down and thanked her God with grateful heart for this mercy that He had shown her. While she knelt and prayed, the constable stood one side and wondered, for he and his were heathen, and so were all the folk of that part of the land.

The constable carried her home to his good wife Hermegild; and those kind people were so grieved to see the stranger's plight that they wept for pity and promised that she might abide with them as long as she would. She would give them no word of who she was or whence she came, but she was so kind and thoughtful and so ready to serve and please all who came near her that everyone who even looked into her face had to love her, whether he would or not. Hermegild loved Constance as her life, and by and by it came to pass that Hermegild and Constance knelt together and offered up their prayers to the God of the Christians.

Now the heathen had overcome all that part of the country, and most of the Christian Britons had fled to Wales. Some few remained here and there in the land, but they did not venture to meet together to worship God, and dared not for their lives avow themselves his followers. Not far from the castle gate were three of these, and one of them was old and blind. One summer's day the constable and Hermegild, his wife, and Constance, his guest, were walking together toward the sea, when they met this blind man, bowed and old and with his eyes tight closed. "For Christ's sweet sake," he cried, "give me my sight again! O Lady Hermegild, open mine eyes for the love of Christ!" Then Hermegild trembled lest her husband should hear the holy name and slay her; but Constance bade her be brave and heal the man if such were God's will. God gave her the power to open the blind man's eyes; and the constable cried in astonishment, "What does this mean?" Constance replied bravely, "Sir, this only shows the power of Christ to help his people out of the control of the evil one." And then she told him of the Christian faith so clearly and so earnestly that before the sun had set, the constable, too, had become Christ's humble follower.

In the town not far from the castle there dwelt a sinful knight, and when Constance refused his wicked love, he swore that she should die, and by a shameful death. One night when the constable was from home, this knight stole like a poisonous serpent to the chamber where Hermegild and Constance lay asleep. He crept softly to the bedside and with a silent stroke he cut the throat of Hermegild. Constance, wearied by her prayers and vigils, slept on quietly, and did not rouse even when the murderer laid the bloody knife close by her side.

The constable made no long tarrying, but came home soon and joyfully, for King Alla was to be his guest. And when he heard the piteous tale, he told it to his King, and also told him of Constance's coming to their land in a strange ship, alone upon the sea. The knight declared that she must have done the cruel deed, and Constance was so overcome with grief and fear and amazement, that she stood almost silent before her judge and had no word to say of her own innocence. Still, when the King looked upon her pure face, he could feel naught but pity. The people, too, declared that she could never have been guilty of such wickedness. "She is pure and good," they said, "and she loved the Lady Hermegild even as her life;" and so said everyone that dwelt in the castle. The King would have proved her innocence or guilt by the test of battle; but the daughter of the mighty Emperor stood alone without a friend to serve her as her champion. The King felt such pity that the tears dropped from his eyes; but justice must be done, and he said, "Bring me a book, and if this knight swear solemnly upon the book that Constance was the slayer of Hermegild, then shall a justice be straightway named to give her trial."

The book was brought, and the knight laid his hand upon it in all boldness. It contained the writings of the four Evangelists; and when the evil man had touched the holy volume and declared on solemn oath that Constance was a murderer, he suddenly fell to the ground like a stone, smitten by an unseen hand; and a voice was heard saying, "Thou hast wronged the daughter of my Holy Church." At such a marvel all the people were aghast, and all save Constance stood in deadly fear of what might happen. Then Constance told the King and all the other folk about the God whom she worshiped; and it came to pass that King Alla and many of the people of the place gave up their heathen worship from that day. The wicked knight was put to death; and when a space of time had passed, King Alla took fair Constance for his wife.

All in the land rejoiced at the marriage save one alone, and that was Donegild, the mother of the King. She was angry that her son should choose for his Queen a strange woman come from no one knew what corner of the world. Nevertheless, there was a wedding and a great feast with dancing and singing. Not long after the wedding King Alla was forced to go to Scotland to meet his enemies in battle. Before he went, he carried his wife to a bishop who was also his constable, and bade him keep watch and ward over her until his return.

Now it came to pass that Constance bore a child, and then the bishop sent a messenger and bade him ride at full speed to carry to his King the blissful news that Constance was the mother of a fair young son. The messenger cared more for his own gain than for his duty, and he said to himself, "If I go out of my way but a little, I can carry the joyful news to the King's mother also, and thus win a double reward." So this faithless servant rode out of his way and went to the home of the King's mother and gave her reverent salutation. "Madame," said he, "I have news to make you happy and blithe, and to make you thank God a hundred thousand times. My lady Queen is the glad mother of a fair young son, and all the land from end to end rejoices. See, madame, here is the sealed letter with the news, and I must bear it as swiftly as I can, that the King, too, may delight in the good tidings. If so be that you would send a message to him, I promise to serve you faithfully both night and day."

Donegild answered, "The hour is late, and I have no letter writ. Tarry, and until the morning take your rest. I will then have ready a message for the King." She plied the messenger with wine and ale, and while he slept the sleep of swine, she stealthily slipped out the letter from his casket and wickedly prepared another to put into its place and signed it with the name of the bishop. This is what the forged letter said: "The Queen has a child, but it is no proper human babe; it is such a horrible, fiendlike creature that no one in the castle dares to stay near it. The mother of such a child is surely nothing less than a fiend."

When the King read this letter, he was sick at heart, but he told no man of his trouble. He wrote a letter to his bishop and gave it to the messenger. Therein he said, "God's will be done. Keep the child, be it foul or fair, and guard my wife till I am again at home. Whatever betide, welcome be the will of God." He sealed this letter, weeping bitter tears of sorrow; and soon the messenger went his way. The faithless servant had no mind to miss the good wine and ale of the King's mother, therefore he went straightway to her abode. She made him welcome as before and did everything that she could to please him and entertain him. He drank as heavily as at his first visit, and again he fell into a swinish sleep. The letter entrusted to his care was stolen from his casket, and in its stead one was placed which said: "The King commands his constable to thrust Constance, once the Queen, from out the kingdom. He is to place her and her child and all that is hers on board the ship on which she came and push it from the shore and charge her that she never again be seen within the limits of the realm. All this he is to do before three days and a quarter of a tide have gone; and if he fail, his head is forfeited."

Such was the letter which the faithless messenger carried to the bishop; and when the good man read it, he cried, "O mighty God, how can it be that thou wilt suffer the innocent to perish and the wicked to prosper? Alas, woe is me! I must either become the executioner of the good Constance or die a shameful death; there is no way of escape."

Throughout the kingdom there was weeping by young and old; but at the dawning of the fourth day Constance, her face as pale as death, went down the path and toward the ship. When she had come to the shore, she knelt upon the sand and prayed, "Lord, whatever thou dost send is always welcome to me," and she said to the sorrowing folk around, "He who cleared me from a false charge when I first came to this land can also care for me on the wide ocean, even though I see not how. He is no less strong than he was before. I trust in him and his Mother, and that trust is for me both rudder and sail." Her little son lay in her arms weeping. "Peace, little son," she murmured; and then she cast her eyes upward to the heavens. "Mother Mary," she cried, "thy Child was tortured on a cross, and thou didst see all his torment. No suffering can compare with thine; for thy Child was slain before thine eyes—and my child lives. O little one," she said to her babe, "what is your wrong? You have never sinned; why will your cruel father take your life?" Then turning to the constable, she pleaded, "O dear kind bishop, can you not let my little child stay here with you? But if you dare not save him from harm, then kiss him once in his father's name." She gave one long look back to the land, said softly, "Farewell, cruel husband!" and walked toward the ship, hushing her child as she went. And when she reached the water's edge, she humbly crossed herself, bade the thronging crowd farewell, and stepped aboard. Food and clothes there were in plenty, for even her merciless enemy dared not send her away without; but she and her babe were on the wide, wide sea with none save Him above to care for them and give them comfort.

Soon after this, King Alla came home and bade the constable send him the Queen and her child. A chill struck to the heart of the good bishop, for he saw that somewhere there had been treachery. He told the King the piteous tale, and said sadly, "Behold, Sir King, your letter and its seal. Grieving, but on pain of death, I have given my best obedience to your will." The King ordered the faithless messenger to be brought before him, and under pain of torture he confessed where he had spent the night when on his way. So, step by step, the King traced out the whole sad story, and knew it was his own mother who, false to the allegiance she had sworn to him and to his rule, had driven his loving wife unto her death. "Be she my mother or my most bitter foe," so said King Alla, "no deed like this shall go unpunished;" and straightway the wicked woman was put to death; but night and day the lonely ruler grieved for wife and child.

Constance for five long years drifted hither and yon upon the sea; but the good Father kept her and her little child in his loving thought, and she was brought safely out of every danger. The ship floated sometimes east and sometimes west; sometimes it turned about and moved north, then, driven by some current or a changing wind, it drifted far to the south. Then through the narrow way between Morocco and the land of Spain it was borne, and far, far to the eastward. Behold, full in its path there came a mighty vessel all bedecked with banners and shields of victors. A Roman senator was in command; and when he saw the lonely woman on the stranger ship, he took her to his own vessel and brought her and her little son in all kind gentleness unto his wife at Rome. Own aunt was the wife to Constance, but the wanderer would tell no story of her past, and so, although for a long while she dwelt in the family of the good senator, no one guessed that she was the daughter of the powerful Emperor.

In faraway Britain the sorrow for her loss was not forgotten. Night and day King Alla mourned for his wife. Then, too, he had other reason for sadness, for he was guilty of his mother's death. At length he made a vow to go to Rome, for he thought that after he had obeyed the Pope's commands in great things and in small, he might dare to hope that Jesus Christ would pardon him his sin.

When it was told in Rome that King Alla was near at hand, then the noble senator and many other men of rank set out with a glittering retinue to meet the royal pilgrim. Many honors were shown him, and to return the courtesies King Alla gave a feast at which all the luxuries of all the world were set forth in abundance. The little son of Constance was to be taken to the feast, and while his mother robed him in his best, she bade him do her will. "Stand in full view of the King," she said, "and look him clearly in the eyes. I thought him once a kindly man; it may be that for you he will have some bit of gentleness even yet;" and then she kissed her child and let him go.

The boy obeyed his mother's word; and Alla, noticing the fair child who gazed at him so eagerly, asked who he was. "That is beyond my power to say," replied the senator. "All I know is that his mother is as good a woman as lives on God's earth;" and then he told the story of how, sailing home in victory from vengeance on the Syrians, inflicted at the Emperor's command, he had met a strange ship with no one on her save this child and a lonely woman.

Straightway King Alla forgot the noble company, forgot the feast, and remembered only how like his lost Queen's face was that of the fair child. "Could the boy's mother be my wife?" he mused, and then he chided himself for his idle folly. "My wife is long since dead," he thought sternly; but into his heart there came the trembling hope, "It was on a lonely vessel that she was brought to my country. May not Christ, who saved her once, have held her in his care a second time?" He could hardly wait for the guests to say farewell; and as soon as they were gone, he hastened homeward with the senator. Constance was bidden to come to meet the King. She stood before him, trembling, swooning, silent, pale as death; for in her heart was the old love of him mingled with sorrow and with just anger at his cruelty, and she had no word to say.

But at the first look King Alla knew his bride. The whole sad tale was told, and the King swore solemnly that, as he hoped for God's mercy on his soul, he was as guiltless of such cruel treachery as was Maurice, their little son. And now, when Constance found she might believe that he was innocent and that his love for her was pure and strong as in the earlier time in faraway Northumberland, there was such happiness in the hearts of those two as never before was felt by mortals in this world. There was even more joy to follow, for at the wish of Constance King Alla made a feast to which the mighty Emperor was humbly bidden. He sent his gracious word of acceptance; and when the day had come, King Alla and Queen Constance rode out in eager thought of happiness at hand to meet their guest. When the Queen looked near upon the Emperor's face, she slipped down from her palfrey and fell meekly at his feet and cried, "Father, I am your Constance. Have you clean forgot your youngest child? I am Constance whom you once sent to Syria. It is I who was thrust out upon the briny sea and doomed to die. Send me no more unto the heathen lands, but thank my lord here for his gentleness."

Sorrow and joy were mingled in the meeting, but soon the sorrow was all forgotten, and never yet was there a feast so glowing with happiness. After many days had passed, King Alla and his Queen returned in joy to their own far kingdom, and there they lived in quiet and peace. And when the time had come for God to take King Alla from the world to his bright heaven, then Constance made her way to Rome, and there, together with her father and her friends of old, she dwelt in holiness and deeds of alms. And when the Emperor had passed away, the child Maurice, now grown a strong and wise and stalwart man, was set upon the throne.

# IV

# The Prioress's Tale

## LITTLE HUGH OF LINCOLN

# The Prioress's Tale

A LL were well pleased with the story told by the man of law. There was some merry jesting about who should tell another tale, but the landlord put an end to it by saying to the prioress with all knightly courtesy, "My lady prioress, if I were sure that it would not give you the least annoyance, I would decree that you should tell the next story. Would you kindly vouchsafe so to do, my dear lady?"

"Gladly," the prioress replied, and without delay began the tale of

## LITTLE HUGH OF LINCOLN

T HERE was once in a great city of Asia a quarter in which the Jews were allowed to live. At the farther end of the street was a school where children were taught to read and to sing. Among these children was a little boy seven years of age, a widow's son, whose name was Hugh. He was so young that he had small book knowledge, but his loving mother had gently taught him whenever he saw the image of the Blessed Mother of Our Lord to kneel before her and say his *Ave Maria* with deepest reverence. So it was that his heart became full of tenderest worship for Our Lady, and as he sat in school with his primer, he listened to the older children singing

*O Alma Redemptoris,* and almost without knowing what he did, he crept nearer and nearer and listened to the words and the music until he knew the first verse and could sing it. Of course he did not know the meaning of the Latin words because he was so young; but he begged an older boy to tell him, and even knelt before him on his little bare knees, so eager was he to know the meaning of the hymn.

At last the older boy said, "Little Hugh, we have been taught that this hymn was written to Our Blessed Lady, and that as we sing it, we are praying her to be our help and comfort when we die. I cannot tell you any more about it, for I am learning singing, not grammar."

"Then if this song was made in honor of Christ's dear Mother," thought the child, "I will surely learn it before Christmas. I will do all I can to show her reverence. Even though I am chidden or even beaten three times in an hour for not studying my primer, I will learn the hymn."

Every day, as they walked home together, the older boy taught little Hugh the hymn, till he knew both words and notes; and then he sang it boldly, loud and clear, both on his way to school and also on his return. *O Alma Redemptoris,* his sweet voice rang out; for his heart was so filled with the love of Christ's dear Mother that he could not cease his singing.

Satan, the evil one, would not endure this song of praise; and he said to the Jews of the quarter, "Will you allow such a thing? Will you permit that boy to go about among you and scoff at you and your laws?"

Thereupon the Jews agreed to do away with the child. There was a wicked murderer who lived in an alley in a dark and secret place, and they hired him to seize the singing child as he passed by and cut his tiny throat and cast his little body down into a pit.

This was why the poor widow waited all night long for her boy to come from school; and when the first ray of light was seen, she started out, her face pale with anxiety and fear, to search for him. She asked at the school and wherever else he was wont to go, calling constantly on Christ's Mother to come to her aid. Finally, she heard that he was last seen going down the street that led through the Jews' quarter, and of every Jew she met she begged piteously, "Can you not tell me anything of my little son?" They answered no, and went their way, not caring for her grief. Still she searched, and the good God put it into her troubled heart to call the name of her lost child near the pit wherein he had been thrown. Here a great miracle was manifested, for down in the deep darkness of the pit the little boy lay; and though his throat was cut by the murderous knife, still he sang loud and clear his *O Alma Redemptoris* till all the place rang with the music.

Many Christian folk were passing through the street, and as the sound of the sweet song came to their ears from that corner of the Jewish quarter, they came pouring in, amazed at such a thing. When they saw the child with his wounded throat, they quickly sent for the provost. He made no delay, but came at once, and after he had given praise to Christ and to his holy Mother, Mary, he bound the Jews with many a bond both strong and firm. He inflicted grievous torture upon them. "Evil to him who deserves evil," he declared; and every guilty man was dragged by wild horses and then hanged upon the gallows tree until his death.

The little martyr child was tenderly lifted up in the midst of piteous weeping and lamentation, and, followed by a long procession of those who wished to do him honor, he was carried to the abbey and laid before the altar. Beside the bier his mother lay swooning with grief; and all this while the sweet voice sang the hymn of praise.

When the mass was done, the abbot cast holy water upon the child to make him ready for his burial, but little Hugh still sang in a sweet, strong voice, *O Alma Redemptoris*. Then said the abbot tenderly, "Dear child, tell me why it is that, though your throat is wounded by the cruel knife, you still sing, *O Alma Redemptoris Mater?*

The child replied, "By nature's way I should have died many hours ago, but Jesus Christ for his own glory and for the worship of his dear Mother has bidden me sing *O Alma* loud and clear. I always loved the Blessed Mother as far as a little child might do, and when I was about to die, she came to me and bade me sing this holy hymn; and then she laid a grain upon my tongue and said to me, 'My little child, when the grain is taken from your tongue, you will call to me no more, for I shall come to carry you away to be with me. Fear not, little one, for I will never forsake you.'"

The holy abbot took away the grain from the child's tongue, and with a little sigh the boy was dead. The abbot and all his monks fell down upon the ground, weeping and wondering and crying praise to Blessed Mary; and then they raised the little martyr from his bier and laid his fair young body in a temple of pure white marble. God grant that we may some day meet him in God's heaven.

# V

# The Nun's Priest's Tale

## THE COCK, THE HEN, AND THE FOX

# The Nun's Priest's Tale

WHEN the prioress had ended her story of little Hugh of Lincoln, the whole company looked thoughtful. This did not suit the cheerful host. He turned to the nun's priest and said, "Come, you Sir John, tell us some pleasant tale to make us merry."

"Yes, mine host," replied the priest. "I will tell a tale, and, by my spurs, it shall be a merry one." Then, without prelude or introduction, he began his story.

## THE COCK, THE HEN, AND THE FOX

ONCE upon a time a poor widow, no longer young, lived in a little cottage in a valley not far from a grove. She had two daughters and only a small income, but she was very economical, and so they managed to live. She cared for three pigs, three cows, and a sheep called Mall. Of course her meals were scanty, but she never needed any pungent sauce to give them flavor, and she was never ill from overeating. If she had wished to dance, the gout would never have prevented her; and surely apoplexy never hurt her head, for she drank neither red wine nor white. The two colors that were oftenest seen on her table were black and white, for there were two things of which she had plenty,—black bread and milk. She had also a bit of broiled bacon now and then, and sometimes an egg or two.

This poor widow had a henyard, and in it she kept a rooster called Chanticleer. There was not another cock in all the land that could crow as well as he. His voice was merrier than the merry organ that plays in the church on mass-days, and one could tell the hour by his crowing better than by any clock. He seemed to know astronomy by nature, for as soon as the sun had risen exactly fifteen degrees, he crowed, and crowed so well that there was no bettering it. He was handsome, too,—by far the handsomest rooster in the place. His comb was redder than the finest coral, and all notched in battlements like a castle wall. His bill was black and shone like jet, his legs and his toes were of a beautiful azure, his nails were whiter than the lily-flower, and his feathers gleamed like burnished gold.

About this cock were seven hens. Their color was much like his, but by far the fairest was Demoiselle Partelote, as she was called. She was so courteous and discreet and such a cheerful companion, and had behaved herself so excellently ever since she was a week old, that Chanticleer loved her with his whole heart, and was never happy away from her. They often sang together, and it was the greatest treat that could be imagined to hear them just at sunrise, when their voices chimed in the song, "My love is far away."

It came to pass one morning early, when Chanticleer was sitting on the perch among his seven wives, that he began to groan as if he was troubled by some bad dream. Partelote sat beside him, of course, and when she heard him groan, she cried, "Sweetheart, what troubles you? What makes you groan?"

The cock replied, "Madame, do not be anxious; it was only a dream, but it was such a terrible one that I am frightened even to remember it. I dreamed that I was walking up and down the yard, when I saw a dreadful creature somewhat like a dog, and it tried to kill me. It was between yellow and red, its tail and ears were tipped with black, its nose was small, and its eyes glowed like fire. That must have been what made me groan, for I am afraid even now."

Then said Dame Partelote, "Fie upon you for a chicken-hearted cock! Pluck up your courage if you would keep my love, for no woman can admire a coward. We long, every one of us, to have a husband who is bold and brave and generous. He must know how to keep a secret, and he must be wise. He must not be frightened at the sight of a knife, and he must not be a braggart. Are you not ashamed to tell your love that you are afraid of anything? You have a beard, haven't you the heart of a man? Dreams are nothing—and to think that you are afraid of them! Dreams often come from overeating and sometimes when one has too much red humor. That would make him see visions of arrows and flames of fire, and red creatures that he fears will bite him. That is what the red humor does, just as the black humor, or melancholy, makes many a man cry out in his sleep for fear of black bears and bulls or black devils. I could tell of more humors that trouble men in sleep. Do you not remember that Cato said, 'Pay no heed to dreams'? Now, dearest," she continued, "when we fly down from here, I pray you take some medicine. There are herbs and berries right in our own yard that will cure you. I will point them out to you."

"Madame," the cock replied, "I thank you for your learning. Cato was a wise man, but there has been many a man of greater wisdom than he who does not agree with him and who has learned by experience that dreams signify either joy or sorrow. One of the most famous authors that men read tells a story of two men who set off together on a pilgrimage. On the way they came to a little village so crowded that there was no room for them both in the same house. One chanced to find a comfortable lodging, but the other could do no better than to lie down in a stall with oxen all about him.

"In the middle of the night the man who was well lodged dreamed that his friend called to him and said, 'Help me, dear brother! Come to me quickly, or I shall be murdered here in an ox's stall.' He woke with a start, and then he thought, 'How foolish to be troubled by a dream!' So he turned over and went to sleep again. The same dream came to him a second time, and a second time he said, 'How foolish!' and went to sleep. A third dream came, and this time the friend did not call for help, but said, 'I have been slain. Look at my gaping wounds. I was murdered for my money.' Then point by point the man told in the dream how it had come about. At last he said, 'If you will get up early in the morning and go to the west gate of the town, you will see a cart full of rubbish. Don't be afraid to stop the cart, for my body will be hidden in the rubbish.'

"This time the man did not say, 'How foolish!' and as soon as it was day, he went to the ox's stall and called for his friend. The innkeeper said, 'Sir, your friend rose early and went out of town.' Then the man went to the west gate, and there he saw a cart of rubbish looking just as his friend had described it in the dream. At this he began to believe the dream must be true. He cried aloud for vengeance. 'My murdered friend lies in this cart!' he declared fearlessly. 'You officers who ought to keep this town, I call upon you for vengeance and justice.' Murder will out. It is such a loathsome thing that God will not suffer it to be concealed. The people gathered all around. They overturned the cart, and in the midst of the rubbish they found the body of the murdered man. Then the officers of the town seized the carter and the innkeeper and tortured them till they confessed the crime, and straightway they were hanged.

"You can see by this that there is truth in dreams. And now in that same book, in the very next chapter beyond this, I read about two men who wanted to cross the sea to a distant country. They waited a long while, for the wind was contrary. At last it changed and blew just as they wished. They planned to start early in the morning, and went to bed happy.

"But while they were asleep a wonderful thing happened, for one of them dreamed that a man stood by his bedside and said, 'If you sail tomorrow, you will be drowned.' He started out of his sleep, called his friend, and told him of the dream. 'Let us put off the voyage for one day,' he said. But his friend only laughed at him for being so foolish as to trust in dreams. 'No dream would ever frighten me,' he declared, 'so that I would give up my business for it. Dreams are only nonsense. People dream of all sorts of wild fancies that never were and never will be. I see, however, that you are bound to stay here and lose the wind. I pity you for your folly, and say farewell.' He went on board the boat and started on his voyage; but before it was half done, something happened, I do not know what, save that the ship sprang a leak and went to the bottom, and the man was drowned. And now, dearest Partelote, you see that one ought not to be careless of dreams. But now let us not talk of this anymore, for when I gaze into your lovely face and see the beautiful scarlet-red about your eyes, I forget all about my fears; I am so happy that I do not care a straw for any dreams or visions."

But now the dawn had come. Chanticleer flew down from the roost and called his hens, and when he had found a kernel of corn, he clucked to them and stood one side to watch them eat it; and certainly no one who saw him looking as brave as a lion and walking up and down the yard on the tips of his toes as if he scorned the ground too much to more than touch it would ever imagine him afraid of anything; and yet trouble lay but a little way before him. As evil fate would have it, there was a wicked fox that had lived for three years in the grove near the cottage. For a long while he had been trying to plan some way to get Chanticleer; and that same night he had slipped softly through a break in the hedge into the yard and had hidden in a bed of cabbages. There he lay, watching with his half-shut eyes the noble rooster walking proudly up and down the yard.

The early morning had passed and nine o'clock had come. Dame Partelote, the beautiful, was bathing in the clean, warm sand, and her sisters were not far away. Chanticleer was singing as merry as a mermaid; but suddenly, while he was watching a butterfly fluttering here and there above the cabbages, he caught sight of the fox lying half hidden among them. His heart turned cold, and the beautiful music of his crowing died in his throat. He cried hoarsely, "Cok! cok! in the greatest fear. In another moment he would have run away, but the fox spoke so gently and courteously that he could not help listening to him. "Gentle sir," said the crafty fox, "I beg of you not to fear so true a friend as I. I should be worse than a fiend to do one like you any harm. I pray you do not think for an instant that I came for any other reason than because I longed so eagerly to hear your singing from nigh at hand that I could not stay away. Indeed, dear sir, you have as sweet a voice as any angel in heaven. Pardon me for addressing you, but, truly, I count myself no stranger to your noble family. My lord, your father—God bless his soul!—and also your mother have honored my poor house by becoming its guests. But to speak again of singing, I never heard anyone except yourself sing so wondrous well as your father used to do at the dawning. He had a habit of making his voice stronger by standing on tip-toe and stretching out his neck. Then he would close his eyes and send forth the sweetest music, save your own, that was ever heard; and as for wisdom and discretion, there was not a person anywhere in the world who could surpass him. Kind sir, would you out of the pure goodness of your heart sing to me once more, and let me fancy that I am listening to your father's voice?"

No one had ever praised Chanticleer so delightfully before. Of course he could not refuse so small a request to one who had shown how fully he enjoyed the best of music. So he stood high upon his toes, stretched out his neck, closed his eyes, and began to crow. His song was, indeed, louder than ever before, so loud that he did not hear the fox stealthily creeping closer to him. And while he was straining his voice till the valley reechoed with his crowing, the treacherous fox caught him by the throat and ran toward the woods, the cock upon his back.

When Troy was burned, the women wept and lamented; but, truly, never before was there heard such crying and screaming as came from the feathered ladies of the yard when they saw the terrible fate that had befallen their noble lord and master. Poor Dame Partelote shrieked louder than all the rest; but the outcries of any one of them might well have reached the skies.

The widow and her daughters heard the alarm and ran to the door. There were the hens and the yard and the grove, and there was the wicked fox, the thief and murderer, running at the top of his speed with the rooster on his back. The women cried, "Stop, stop! a fox, a fox!" and ran after him as fast as they could go. The men caught up sticks and ran; the dog Coll ran; and Talbot and Garland and Malkin with a distaff in her hand; the cow and the calf ran; and even the hogs, for they were so frightened at the shouting of the people and the barking of the dogs that they ran, squealing all the way like very fiends. The ducks quacked as if they thought men were trying to kill them; the geese squawked, took wing, and flew over the tops of the trees; and a swarm of bees came buzzing out of their hives and flew after them. And this was not all, for the people ran home to get trumpets of brass and boxwood and horn and bone. They bellowed, they blew, they shouted, they bawled, they hooted and roared and yelled and howled and screeched and screamed, till they raised such a hullaballoo as was never heard on the earth before—and all this time the fox was running toward the wood with the cock on his back.

Some folk behave better when they are in trouble than when all goes smoothly with them, and Chanticleer was one of these people. He knew well that the fox could reach his hole before the pursuers could catch up with him, and that whatever was done must be done at once. He had grown far wiser since he had been taken prisoner, and he said calmly to his captor, "Sir, if I were you, I would defy all that rabble. I would say to them, 'Turn back, proud men, a plague upon you all! I am close to the grove, and I will eat the cock in spite of you.'"

"In faith," declared the fox, "that is the very thing I will do." But the cock was ready, and the instant the fox opened his mouth to speak, he broke loose, flapped his wings, and in another moment he was perched high upon a tree.

The fox was too wily to be put out of countenance by even such a surprise as this. He looked up meekly into the tree and said in a humble voice, "My dear Chanticleer, I am heartily ashamed of myself; and I beg your pardon most submissively. I ought to have remembered that you were not used to my ways and not to have startled you so when I brought you out of your yard. Honestly, sir, I never thought of doing you harm. If you will kindly come down to the ground where we may talk more comfortably, I shall be glad to explain the matter to you."

"No, sir," replied the cock, with just a bit of an exultant crow; "may the fiends take me if you cheat me more than once. You will not get me to sing and shut up my eyes again, for no one will ever thrive who shuts up his eyes when he ought to keep them open."

"Not that," replied the fox, "but bad luck to him who talks when he ought to hold his peace."

Thus ends the story of the cock and the hen and the fox.

# VI

## The Pardoner's Tale

### THE REVELERS WHO WENT OUT TO MEET DEATH

# The Pardoner's Tale

"THAT was, indeed, a merry tale," cried Harry Bailey. "And now, you pardoner," he continued, "do you, too, set to work to amuse us. Tell us some story of mirth and jesting, and see you to it that you entertain us well."

"Surely, but I must first step into yonder inn and have a bite of cake and a drink or two."

But the pilgrims cried, "No, we do not want any barroom stories. Tell us a tale with a good moral."

"Of course I will," declared the pardoner, "but I must have my drink; and while I am drinking, I will think up some good honest story." So the pardoner went into the tavern; and when he came out, this is the story that he told.

## THE REVELERS WHO WENT OUT TO MEET DEATH

THERE once lived in Flanders a company of wild young men who gave themselves up to foolish revelry. Day and night they rioted. They gambled, they gorged themselves with the richest viands, they drank till they could not have told whether they were men or beasts, and they swore such terrible oaths that it would freeze one's blood to hear them.

My story is a truly moral tale about three of these revelers who sat together in a tavern one morning. It was not yet nine o'clock, but these young rioters did not even await the coming of night for their orgies; and though it was so early, they had already emptied many cups. The tinkling of a bell was heard from the street. "What's that?" one asked, and another replied, "Nothing but the jingling of a bell before a corpse."—"Boy," the first called tipsily to the waiter, "do you go and ask the corpse's name; and see that you don't forget it on the way back."

"Sir, there is no need of asking," the boy replied, "for I knew two hours and more ago who was to be buried this morning; and surely there is no need of telling you, for he was an old companion of yours. He was sitting on a bench dead drunk last night, and a sly old thief that they call Death came upon him suddenly and thrust a spear through his heart, and the man fell over dead. That old fellow kills all the people in the country hereabouts; he struck down a thousand the last time of pestilence. My mother used to tell me to see to it well that I was ready to meet him."

"The boy tells the truth," declared the tavern-keeper. "Why, in the great village over yonder, only a mile from here, Death has slain man, woman, child, page, and hind within this one year. I believe he lives there. My word upon it, it needs a pretty wise man to be on his guard against him."

"And you call it such a peril to meet him?" said one of the revelers. "I tell you I'll go to seek him by street and by lane, I vow I will. Listen to me, fellows, we are all agreed. Let us each hold up his hand and swear that we will stand by one another like brothers and kill this traitor Death. He has slain many, but before night he'll be dead himself; he will."

So the three, all of them half drunk, swore tipsily that they would be as true to one another as born brothers, and then they staggered toward the village that the tavern-keeper had pointed out to them; and as they walked they swore many dreadful oaths that if they could only catch this Death, they would surely kill him.

Before they had gone half a mile, they came to a stile, and on the other side of the stile was an old man in poor and worn-out garments. He tottered out of their way and said meekly, "God keep you, gentlemen."

The proudest of the revelers glanced at him and laughed scornfully. "Old fellow," he said, "why do you keep yourself all wrapped up except your face? Why do you keep on living any longer when you are so old?"

The old man looked him straight in the eyes and replied, "I am old because I cannot find a man who will give me his youth and take my age. Whether I went to city or country or even to faraway India, it would be the same; and so I must keep my age as long as it is God's will. Neither, alas, will Death take my life. That is why I wander about, a restless, miserable wretch. The first thing in the morning and the last thing at night I knock on the ground with my staff, for the ground is the gate to my mother's house; and I cry, 'Dear mother, let me in! See how thin I am! Flesh and skin and blood have withered away. When will my old bones find rest? I would gladly give up to you all that I have if you would but give me a shroud to wrap me in.' She will not do me the favor, and that is why my face is so pale and wrinkled. But, sirs, it is no honor to you to speak so roughly to an old man who has done nothing to harm you. If you stay in this world, you, too, will soon be old; and I counsel you not to do to any old man what you would not wish to have done to you when you are old. Farewell, sirs, and God be with you whether you ride or walk. I must go on my way."

"Hold on, old fellow," cried one of the revelers. "You won't get off so easily as that. You talk about this rascally Death, who is always murdering our friends about here. I believe you are his spy, and now if you don't tell us where to find him, it will be the worse for you, understand that; for I have no doubt at all that you are in league with him to slay us young folk."

The old man replied, "Sirs, if you want to find Death so badly, certainly I can tell you which way to go. Do you see that little winding path that leads into the woods? I saw him there just now, sitting under an oak tree. He will stay, depend upon it. He'll not run away from you for all your boasting. God save you, and make you mend your ways!"

The tipsy revelers hurried to the tree to find Death. He was not to be seen, but on the ground there lay a great heap of golden florins, bushels of them, all bright and shining as if they had just been coined. The three men threw themselves down upon the pile of gold, they felt of it, they let it run through their fingers, they held up handfuls of it to see it glitter in the sunshine. After a while the worst villain among them said, "Brothers, you know that I make merry and jest, but I have some wisdom for all that. Now listen to what I say. Here is this great heap of gold, and it is plain enough that our lucky stars have sent it to us that we might have a jolly time all the rest of our lives. And that we will," he swore by a terrible oath. "Who would ever have dreamed that such a thing as this would have come to us! But now listen! This gold must be taken care of, and we might count ourselves in luck if it were safely stored away in either my house or yours; but how are we going to get it there? We cannot carry it by daylight, for someone would be sure to see us, and then the officers would say we were thieves, and they would hang us for taking care of our own gold. We must carry it in the night, that is sure, and be sly about it at that; and we must keep watch of it all day or else some thief will find it and steal it from us. Now hear my plan. We will draw lots, and the one to whom the lot falls shall run to the town as fast as ever he can and secretly get some bread and wine. While he is gone, the other two shall keep close watch and ward; and then, if all goes well, as soon as night comes, we will carry the treasure wherever we may decide will be the safest place."

The others agreed to this plan, and they drew lots. The lot fell to the youngest, and he ran off cheerfully all the way to the town; but long before he reached it, he, too, had a plan in his head.

The two who were left behind sat them down beside the gold; but even while they could still hear the footsteps of him who had gone to the town, the worst villain said to the other, "You know that you and I have sworn to be brothers, and so I am going to tell you something that will greatly advantage you. Now here is a great heap of gold, but when it is divided among three of us, the heaps will be much smaller. If I could manage matters so it need only be divided between us two, shouldn't I be doing you a favor?"

"In faith you would," the other replied; "but I don't see how you would set about it. He knows that the gold was here when he left us, and what could we say to him?"

"Will you vow to keep the plan secret?" demanded the first villain. "If you will, I can tell you in two words how to bring it about."

"I vow," declared the second villain, "that, whatever comes, I will never betray you."

The first villain bent himself across the heap of gold and drew the other villain nearer to him, and then he whispered in his ear, "There are two of us, and two are stronger than one—now do you understand? This will be the way. When he comes, do you begin a friendly wrestling match. While you are wrestling as if in sport, I will slip up behind him and thrust my knife into his side. Then do you draw out your dagger and do the same. And then, my dear, true friend, we shall have all this gold for our two selves. We can drink the rarest wines, we can gamble as much as we will, and all our lives long we shall be free to do as we list."

So it was that the two villains plotted to kill the third.

But the third had also a thought in his head, as I have said before, and no matter how fast he ran, his wicked scheme grew faster. "Oh, the gold, the gold," he said to himself. "If I could only have it all for my own, I should be the happiest man in the world; but there's no way out of it, two parts must go to them, and only one to me." And then he, too, made an evil plan. He hurried to an apothecary and said, "Sir, I am so troubled with rats that I do not know what to do. Can you sell me a poison that will make way with them?"

"That I can," replied the apothecary. "Here in this cabinet I keep a powder, and if you should give a bit of it no larger than a grain of wheat to any creature on the earth, he would fall down dead before you had walked a mile."

The villain went away from the apothecary with some of the poison safely stored away in a little box. He went next to a man who lived close by, and borrowed three large wine bottles and filled them with wine. Into two of them he put the poison, but the third he kept free for his own drinking that night. "For I shall have to labor and toil all night long," he said to himself, "to get the gold safely stored away in my house before daylight."

So it was that the two plans were laid, and it came to pass that both of them were carried out. The two villains who had stayed in the woods to watch the gold began the wrestling, and in it killed the third just as they had plotted. Then they sat down to make merry and to drink the wine; and in less time than one could walk a mile they both lay dead. This was the end of the revelers who set out to find Death, for so it was that they found him.

# VII

# The Wife of Bath's Tale

## THE UNKNOWN BRIDE

# The Wife of Bath's Tale

THE next pilgrim called upon for a tale was the wife of Bath. She chose to tell one of the days of King Arthur.

## THE UNKNOWN BRIDE

IN the olden times, many hundred years ago, the whole land was full of fairies. They were on the hills and in the valleys, and whoever went to any green meadow was sure to see the elf-rings where the fairy queen and her merry rout had been dancing the night before. There are no fairies now; and if you go where they used to be, you will be sure to see a begging friar roaming up and down the land, but never a fairy.

Now in the times when there were fairies everywhere, it came to pass that a knight who dwelt at King Arthur's court forgot his vow to guard all women and treated one despitefully. The law was that any knight so faithless to his word should straightway be put to death; but this knight was a favorite at the court, and every one of the court ladies, from the Queen down, pleaded that his life might be spared. They begged King Arthur for mercy so often and so earnestly that at length he said, "I will give him to the Queen, and he may live or die according to her will."

The Queen and all her ladies thanked the King; and then the Queen said to the guilty knight, "It is true that we have besought the King for you, but your life is not yet sure. It is not right that you should go unpunished. The rope is even now about your neck, but on one condition you shall be free. If in a year and a day you can tell me what it is that women wish for most, then your life shall be spared."

The knight took his leave of the Queen and the court and went his way to find out what women wish for most. He roamed the world over and asked everyone that he met. They all had answers, some of them most excellent ones, but the trouble was that no two agreed. One said women cared most for riches, another said for honor, another for merriment, another for brilliant attire, another for praise, another for freedom. One even insisted that a woman would rather keep a secret than do anything else; but of course that is nonsense, for we women cannot conceal things. Don't you know Ovid's story of King Midas? He had a pair of asses' ears, but he contrived to hide them so well under his long hair that no one in the world except his wife knew they were there. He begged her most earnestly not to let anyone know the secret, and she promised that if the whole world were offered her, she would never reveal it. She meant to keep her word; but that secret bubbled and swelled so about her heart that she felt she could not live without telling someone. She did not dare tell it to any person, and so she slipped away to a marsh that was full of reeds. She stooped and put her mouth down close to the water and whispered, "O water, I am going to tell you a secret, but don't you ever let anyone know it: my husband has two long asses' ears!" There you see that we women cannot keep a secret.

But to go back to the knight. When he found that, go where he would and ask whom he would, no two persons agreed in their answers, he was sorrowful indeed; for if not even two people thought the same, there was no hope that he had found the answer which would save his neck from the rope. But the day had come when he must return, or else his sureties would be put to death in his place. He turned about sadly, and with many a sigh he rode along by the edge of a forest. As he cast his eyes a little way ahead, he saw full four and twenty ladies dancing gayly on a little green. "Perhaps they are some of the wise folk and can give me the answer," he said to himself, and he hastened toward them eagerly. But, alas, before he had come to the dance, the ladies had all disappeared, and in their place was one old crone, bent and bowed and more hideous than he had ever imagined a woman could be. When he came nearer, she rose slowly and clumsily to her feet and said, "Sir knight, there is no road here. What are you in search of? We old folk know a good many things, and it may be better for you to tell me what you want."

The knight was so miserable that he was glad to tell his trouble to anyone who would listen, and he said, "Good mother, if you could only tell me what it is that women want most, I would reward you well, for I am a dead man if I cannot find out."

"What women want most?" repeated the old crone. "There is no difficulty about telling that. See, we will make a bargain. I will tell you the answer if in return you will agree to do the first thing I ask of you."

"By my faith as a knight I promise you," he said; and, indeed, he was so wretched that he would have promised anything to anyone who would give him the slightest hope of safety.

The woman said, "Cheer up, cheer up, my good knight. Your life is safe; for I will wager my own that the humblest and the proudest, the poorest and the richest, even the Queen herself, will have to say that I am right. Don't be afraid; this is your answer," and she whispered a few words into his ear.

It was not long before the knight came to the palace, and sent a message to the Queen that he had kept his day faithfully and was ready with his answer. A time was set, and all the ladies of the court, maidens, wives, and widows, came together to hear what answer he would give. The Queen sat on a dais with the court ladies around her. There was no need of calling for silence, for everyone there was holding her breath and straining her ears to hear what the knight would say. He walked into the room with his head held up fearlessly, and bowed low before the Queen.

"Tell me," she said, "what it is that women most desire."

There was no need that the court ladies should strain their ears, for the knight answered in a clear, manly voice, "The thing that women most desire is to rule their husbands. This is their strongest wish. I declare it even though you put me to death. I am at your mercy. Do with me as you will."

There was not one court lady present who would deny the truth of what he had said. They all agreed that he ought to have his life, and the Queen at once declared that he was free of every bond and claim.

"No, my lady Queen," said a strange voice. "I beg your mercy, but there is yet a claim upon him. Give me justice, I pray, before you depart. I told the knight what answer to make, and in return he vowed by his knightly faith that he would do the first thing I should ask of him if it were in his power. Now before this court I demand, sir knight, that you take me for your own wedded wife. You know well that I saved you from the gallows tree. If I speak falsely, deny this upon your faith."

"Alas," said the knight, "I know only too well that such was my promise; but for God's sake make another choice. Take all my wealth if you will, but let me go free."

"No," she replied. "I am old and homely and poor, but for all the gold that is buried in the earth I would not give up being your wife and your love."

"My love? Rather, my ruin," said the knight. "Alas, that such a thing should be, that such a shame should befall my house!" There was no help for it, however, he must take the old crone for his wife, and so he married her; but you may know well that there was no merriment and no feasting at that wedding.

After the wedding, the knight was so glum and serious that the bride said, "Is this the way King Arthur's knights behave with their brides? I am your love and your wife, and, surely, I have never done you a wrong. Did I not save your life? Why do you treat me so? If I have done anything unkind to you, tell me what it is, that I may make all the amends in my power."

"Amends!" cried the knight. "There are no amends that can be made, for you come of such common folk, and you are so poor and old and homely."

Then the bride told him that folk might indeed hand down their wealth to their children, but not their goodness; that a man is not noble because he is the son of a duke or an earl, but because he himself does noble deeds. "I am of gentle blood," she said, "if I live virtuously and do not sin. And as for my poverty," she continued, "it is true that a man would never choose to be poor; but, nevertheless, he who is poor need have no dread of thieves. Poverty is like a glass through which one may see who are his true friends; and sometimes poverty teaches a man to know both his God and himself. You call me old, but is it not true that gentle folk of honor and courtesy never fail to show respect to age? Often it happens that with age comes wisdom."

The knight could not help seeing that her words were wise and true, and when she asked, "Would you rather have me old and poor and homely and come of common folk, but a faithful, loving wife; or, perchance, young and rich and handsome and of high birth, but careless of your love and maybe false to you?" he pondered and sighed, and sighed and pondered; and at last he said, I believe that you are wise and good, and I take you for my true and faithful wife."

"On my word I will be to you as true a wife as ever lived since the world was made," declared his bride. "Now kiss me once and then draw up the curtain."

The knight obeyed; and when he had drawn up the curtain and turned his eyes upon her in the full sunlight, behold, she was young and fair and charming. He caught her in his arms and kissed her, not once, but a thousand times, and then a thousand more; and unto the last day of their lives they lived in peace and happiness.

# VIII

## The Friar's Tale

### THE STORY OF THE SUMMONER

# The Friar's Tale

W HEN the friar's turn had come, he told a tale about a certain summoner, whose business it was to summon to the archdeacon's court all those in his jurisdiction who were accused of breaking the laws of the Church. The archdeacon did not always know how much this summoner was getting from the people, for the man would often threaten them without ground or reason, and to get rid of being called before the court they were right glad to fill his purse or make him great feasts at the alehouse.

## THE STORY OF THE SUMMONER

N ow it came to pass one day that a summoner wanted a little money, so he set out to summon an old widow. As he rode along by the forest, he saw riding before him a gay young yeoman with bright new bow and arrows. He wore a short coat of black and a hat with black fringe.

"Sir," said the summoner, "greeting and good cheer to you."

"Welcome," returned the stranger, "to you and to every good fellow and true. Whither go you under this green shade? Do you ride far today?"

"Oh, no," the summoner answered; "I am only going right here to collect a rent for my lord."

"Ah, you are a bailiff, then?"

"Yes, truly," he replied, for he was ashamed to own that he was a summoner.

"Then are we both bailiffs," said the yeoman. "I am a stranger in this part of the country, and I shall be glad of your acquaintance, of your brotherhood, too, if so be you are of like wish. If you ever chance to come into my shire, you will find that I have plenty of gold and silver in my chest, and whatever of it you may need shall be your own, I promise you that."

The summoner thanked the stranger heartily. The two men grasped each other's hands and vowed to be sworn brethren to the last day of their lives; and then they rode on, talking pleasantly together.

The summoner was full of chatter, and he was never done with his questioning. "Brother," he asked, "where do you live? Where should I look for you if I would find you some other day?"

The yeoman replied to him smoothly and politely. "Far in the north country," he said, "where I hope, my brother, I shall some time see you. Before we separate, I will tell you the way so carefully that you will never miss my house."

Then the summoner introduced a new subject. "Now, brother," said he, "since you are a bailiff as well as I, I beg you to tell me some trick that will help me to get the most money from my office. No matter whether it is right or wrong, but tell me as a brother how you manage matters."

"Now by my truth, dear brother," replied the other, "I will tell you an honest tale. My lord is stingy and close-fisted, and I have a hard place. Therefore I live by getting just as much from every man as he can be made to give. I get my pay either by trick or by force; but I get it, you may depend upon that."

"That is my way, too," said the summoner. "I take everything I can lay hold of unless it is too heavy or too hot. I could not live in any other way; and there's one thing more, I won't tell of this in confession. We are well met, I am sure; but, dear brother, tell me your name, I pray."

The yeoman smiled a queer little smile. "Brother," said he, "do you really want me to tell you? Then here it is—I am a fiend, and my dwelling-place is hell. I am riding about to gather in whatever I can, for this is all my income. You don't care how you get your money, and neither do I. I would ride to the end of the earth for my prey."

"Ah," said the summoner, "how is this? I certainly thought you were a yeoman. You have a man's form as much as I. Do you have a form when you are at home in hell?"

"No, we have none there," the fiend replied; "but we can take one whenever we choose, or we can make anyone think that we have the form of a man or an ape, or an angel for that matter. That is nothing wonderful. A common juggler can cheat you, and surely I have more skill than he."

The summoner would have gone on asking question after question, but the fiend gently cut him short. "Hereafter, my dear brother," he said, "you shall come where you will not need to learn of me. Now let us ride on briskly, for you may be sure that I shall stay with you unless you leave me."

"Oh, no," declared the summoner, "that will never come to pass. We have sworn to be brothers, and I will keep my word, even though you were Satan himself. You take all you can get, and I will do the same; and if either of us gets more than the other, then let him share."

"Agreed, by my faith," declared the fiend; and then they rode on together to the edge of the town where the summoner had planned to go. In the road was a cart loaded with hay, and it bade fair to stand in the road for some time to come; for the mud was so deep that, try as they would, the horses could not stir it. The carter beat them and shouted as if he were mad. "Go on, Scot! Get up, Brok! The fiend take you, and the cart and hay, too!"

"Here's somewhat for you," said the summoner softly to the fiend. "Listen, brother, listen! Don't you hear what the carter says? Take it; he has given it all to you, hay and cart and his three good horses."

"No," the fiend responded, "I cannot take that, because he doesn't mean it in earnest. Ask him for yourself, if you doubt me, or else wait a little and you will see."

The carter struck his horses another blow, and they began to pull harder than ever. "Get up!" he cried. "There, we are out of it at last. That was well done, old Gray. God save thee, and bless everything that He ever made!"

"Now, brother," said the fiend, "now, you see, I cannot get anything from this wagon; so let us go on farther."

They passed on through the town. When they came near to the end, the summoner whispered to the fiend, "My brother, an old woman lives in yon small house who would about as soon lose her neck as give up a penny. I will have twelve pence out of her, though, if she goes mad, or I will summon her to our court. I don't know any wrong of her, but no matter. Now watch me, brother; and since you do not seem to know how to get what belongs to you in this country, you can follow my example and learn from me."

The summoner knocked loud at the widow's gate. "Come out," he called, "come out."

"Who is that?" asked the woman. "Ah, God save you, sir, what is your will?"

"I have here," replied the summoner, "a bill requiring you to appear at the archdeacon's court tomorrow morning to answer to certain charges made against you."

"I call God to witness," declared the woman, "that I cannot. I have been sick for a long while, and my side pains me so that I can neither ride nor walk. Sir summoner, may not one appear for me at the court and answer there to whatever thing is charged against me?"

"Yes," replied the summoner; "pay me twelve pence, and I will see to the matter. I shall get small gain from it; my master has the profit, not I. Come, give me the twelve pence, and let me ride on. I can't wait here any longer."

"Twelve pence!" cried the widow. "I've not twelve pence to my name. You know right well that I am poor and old. Have pity on me in my trouble."

"Never," declared the summoner. "May the fiend take me if I let you off, even if it ruins you."

"Alas," she wailed, "God knows I have done nothing wrong."

"Pay the twelve pence," growled the summoner, "or I will carry away your new pan for the debt that you owed me before."

"You say false," she shrieked. "Never in all my life was I summoned to your court till now. May the fiend take you, and my pan too."

When the fiend heard this, he drew nearer. "Good mother," he asked gently, "do you really mean what you are saying?"

"May the fiend take him, pan and all, if he does not repent!" repeated the old woman.

"Repent, indeed!" cried the summoner. "I'll not repent of taking anything from you. I wish I had everything that belongs to you."

"Now, brother," said the fiend, "don't be angry, but you and this pan are mine by right, and this very night you shall go to my dwelling in hell with me;" and with that the fiend caught him and bore him away, body and soul, to the place where folk like him have heritage prepared.

# IX

## The Clerk's Tale

### PATIENT GRISELDA

# The Clerk's Tale

THE clerk had been riding along quietly, and apparently thinking about something other than the stories that the rest of the company were telling. Suddenly the host turned toward him and said, "Sir clerk of Oxford, you ride along as shy as a young wife sitting at the table with her husband for the first time. I have not heard a word from you today. I suppose you are pondering over some deep question or other, but Solomon said there was a time for everything, and be sure of it, this is not the time to study. When a man has begun a game, he ought to play it. Come, then, tell us a good story. Don't preach us a sermon, and don't put us to sleep, but tell us a cheerful, wide-awake tale of adventures. Keep your fine rhetoric and your logic to use when you are writing in lofty fashion as one would write to a king; and talk to us plainly enough so we can understand you."

The clerk replied with full courtesy, "My host, I am at your service. You are our governor, and certainly I would pay my best obedience to you. I will tell you a story that I once heard at Padua from a worthy clerk named Francis Petrarch. He is dead now. God grant peace to his soul."

# PATIENT GRISELDA

IN the western part of Italy there is a broad, sunny plain, rich and fertile, and scattered over it are many ancient towns whose towers were founded in the days of our ancestors. A certain marquis named Walter was ruler of this land, as his forefathers had been before him. He was honest and courteous, and he ruled his country well. His people feared him and obeyed him, but they loved him, too, and they dreaded to have the time come when he would no longer be their lord. They wished most earnestly that he would marry. "If he only had a son," they said, "who would follow in his father's footsteps, we should feel at rest;" but the Marquis showed no wish to marry. He was young and strong and was enjoying himself so much with his hunting and hawking and other pleasures that he was inclined to let matters slide, and come what might, he would not take a wife.

The people talked the question over, and at length one of the wisest among them said, "Let us go to the Marquis and tell him humbly how much we honor him and love him and how it would grieve us if his line should fail and some stranger come to take the rule over us."

This was agreed to, and soon a number of the Marquis's subjects went to see him. One man to whom he had shown special favor acted as spokesman. He told his lord how the people felt, and begged him earnestly, though with all meekness, that he would permit them to choose him a wife from among the noblest of the land.

The Marquis could not help being touched by the faithfulness of his people in their love for him, and he promised to take a wife. Then he said to them, "I had never thought of being married, but now that I am giving up my freedom at your request, I ask something of you in return. I will choose a wife for myself wherever my heart may be set—you need not be burdened with that charge—and I ask you to swear to me most solemnly that, whatever wife I may select, you will neither carp nor cavil at my choice. And, furthermore, I must also have your sworn promise that, whoever she may be, you will show her the reverence and respect which you would show to the daughter of an emperor, and that this shall never fail so long as her life shall endure."

The people were ready enough to take the oath; but even then they were afraid that month after month would slip by and the Marquis would still delay his marriage; therefore they knelt before him even more humbly and begged that he would of his great goodness add to the kindness he had already shown them by setting a day for his wedding. The Marquis named a day, and promised that without fail he would take to himself a wife when that time should come. The people thanked him over and over again, and then went joyfully to their homes, while the Marquis sent for his officers and bade them see to it that on that day a noble wedding feast should be made ready.

Not far from the splendid palace of the Marquis there was a little village where only poor folk lived. The poorest of them all was a man named Janicula; but he was rich in one respect, for he had a fair young daughter named Griselda. She was not only beautiful, but she was industrious and good, and she did everything in her power to help her poor old father. They had a few sheep, and when she went out to watch them, she always carried her distaff with her that she might spin as she watched. On her way home she gathered roots and herbs to cook for their frugal meals; and in everything she gave her father loving care and reverence and honor.

The Marquis had often noticed this young girl as he was on his way to the hunt. He saw how womanly she was, and he noted what the people in the village said of her goodness. He often thought of her face, not only beautiful but pure and strong and true, and he had resolved that if ever he married anyone, this young girl should be his wife.

Day after day passed. Lavish preparations for the wedding were going on at the palace. The country had been scoured for dainty viands, the whole house had been put in order and arranged as handsomely as a house may be. The Marquis had sent his messengers to other lands for gems whereof to make rings and brooches and necklaces and bracelets. He had even had many rich and costly garments made to the measure of one of the court ladies who was much the height and figure of the humble village maiden.

The wedding day had come, but even then no one knew who was to be the bride; and the people began to wonder secretly whether after all the Marquis was only making fools of them. The lords and ladies had come to the wedding. The Marquis in his richest array came forward to give them greeting. "But before we seat ourselves at the feast," he said, "we will ride a little way to the small village near at hand."

So all the splendid assembly set out for the little village, wondering and wondering what wild whim the Marquis had in his mind. It was a brilliant company, and as they rode along the way was bright with velvet and satin and cloth of gold, with rubies and emeralds and diamonds and all the other beautiful adornments that the wedding guests had provided to do honor to the Marquis and the high-born maiden whom he would of course choose for his bride.

Not only the people who lived in great houses were interested in the marriage, but also the folk of every tiny hamlet, and naturally the maiden Griselda. When she heard that the Marquis and his guests were on their way, she hurried to finish her morning's work, so that she would have time to stand in the doorway with the other young girls and see the new Marchioness, if the wedding party should chance to return that way. She was just bringing a waterpot of water from the well when the Marquis called, "Griselda." She set down the waterpot and fell upon her knees before him to hear what his will might be. "Griselda," he said, "where is your father?"

She replied humbly, "Lord, he is here;" then went into the cottage and brought her father out.

The Marquis dismounted and left the glittering rout. He took the old man's hand and led him to one side. "Janicula," he said, "I can no longer hide the wish of my heart. If you will grant me leave, I will take your daughter for my wife before I go from this place, and mine she shall be so long as her life shall endure. I know well that you love me and have been my faithful liegeman all your days. Tell me, then, are you willing to take me as your son-in-law?"

It is no wonder that Janicula was so amazed that he turned first red, then white, and then stood silent and trembling. At last he spoke, but in so low a voice that the Marquis could barely hear him say, "Whatever you will, I will. You are my lord; do in this matter according to your pleasure."

"My will is, then," said the Marquis gently, "that I and you and she confer together in your house in order that you may hear all that is said. I will ask her in your presence if she is willing to become my wife and to obey my wish in all things."

The humble village maiden was not used to so lordly a guest, and it is small wonder that her face was pale. The Marquis took her by the hand and said, "Griselda, I wish to take you for my bride. This will be pleasing to your father, and, I suppose, to you; but first I want your free answer to what I ask. If you become my wife, do you promise to do my will and never grumble, whether I give you pleasure or pain? Do you promise that when I say yes, you will never say no, either by words or by a frown? Swear this, and here I swear to take you for my wife."

Griselda was trembling with fear and wonder, but she answered, "Lord, I am not worthy of such an honor; but if this is your will, it is also mine. I swear that I will die rather than willingly disobey you in deed or in thought."

"Enough, my Griselda," said the Marquis. He passed out of the door, the maiden following him with modest, downcast face, and there they stood in full view of the noble company of guests. While the guests gazed and wondered, and, turning aside, smiled scornfully, he said in a loud, clear voice, "This maiden is to be my wife. If anyone claims to honor me and love me, let him honor her and love her. There is no more to be said about it."

Then the beautiful new robes were brought out that the Marquis had had made, and the haughty court ladies had to go into the tiny cottage and dress the humble village maiden in the velvets and satins. They combed and braided her hair and set a crown upon her head and loaded her with jewels rich and rare. Then they led her out before the people; and her beauty was so brought out by all this brilliant attire that even the folk of her own village almost doubted that this was she.

The Marquis wedded her with a ring that he had brought with him, and set her upon a snow-white horse, and they rode on to the castle. The retinue grew longer all the way, for the story of the marriage had gone before them, and the people of every little village through which they passed turned out to do honor to the child of their own people who had now become their Marchioness. When the company reached the palace, the feasting began, and the revels lasted till the very setting of the sun.

To make a long story short, God gave such grace to the new Marchioness that no one who looked upon her would have fancied that she had grown up in a cottage, but rather in the palace of an emperor. Everyone loved her and reverenced her, and even the people who had known her ever since she was born could hardly make themselves believe that she was the daughter of their simple, honest neighbor Janicula. The report of her great excellence spread not only through Saluces, but through other countries, and many people came long distances merely to look upon her face. Not only could she rule her house well, but if any trouble arose among the people of the land, she was so wise and so just that she always succeeded in bringing them to peace; and, indeed, more than one man declared that she had surely been sent from heaven to right every wrong. After a while a daughter was born to her, and then the palace was even happier than before. So it came to pass that the Marquis and his wife of humble birth lived together in peace and joy. "He could see goodness and prudence in a maid of low degree," said the people; "he is a wise man;" and they loved their lord more than ever.

When the baby was only a few months old, a foolish thought came into the heart of the Marquis. He longed to test his wife's steadfastness, and see whether she would keep the promises that she made him on their wedding day. So he came to her one night with a stern and troubled face, and asked, "Griselda, do you remember the day when I took you out of your poverty and made you a marchioness? Now listen to every word that I say. You are dear to me as ever, but not to my nobles. They say it is shameful for them to have to be subject to you and to serve one of such humble birth. They have said this more and more since your daughter was born; and now, if I would live my life in peace, I am forced to do with the child not what I would choose, but what they demand. I will do nothing without your knowledge and consent; but I require of you now to obey my will with the patience and obedience that you promised on our marriage day."

Griselda's face did not change, and not a tear did she shed, even though her heart was breaking. She replied humbly, "Lord, my child and I are yours, and surely you may do with your own as you will. Whatever pleases you pleases me. There is nothing in the world that I dread except to lose you."

The Marquis was delighted at her words, but he kept on his sober face, and left the room. There was in his service a man whom he could trust to do either good or evil without a question, whichever he was bidden. The Marquis gave him his orders, and in a short while he burst into the room of the Marchioness and said roughly,

"Madame, you will have to pardon me, but you are so wise that you must know that whatever Lord Walter commands has to be done. I am bidden to take that child away."

The knave looked as if he were ready to slay the baby before its mother's eyes; and yet Griselda sat meek and still, and did not even weep. At last she asked humbly, "May I kiss my child before it dies?" She sadly held the little one to her heart, and soothed it and kissed it. Then she made the sign of the cross upon it and said a blessing over it. She spoke to it gently. "Farewell, my little girl," she whispered. "I shall never see you again. May God bless you, little child, for tonight you must die for my sake." Then to the officer she said meekly, "I give you back your little one. Go now and do as my lord commanded you; but if he does not forbid, I beg you in mercy to bury this little body in some place where neither beasts nor birds of prey will find it and tear it in pieces." The officer made no reply. He caught up the child roughly and went his way.

When he stood before his lord with the child in his arms, the Marquis said, "Wrap the child up warmly and carry it gently to my sister, the Countess of Pavia. Tell her to care for it with all kindness, but never to let it be known whose child it is. And, sirrah," he continued, "if you wish to keep your head on your shoulders, see to it that no one finds out where you are going or what you are carrying."

The officer went to obey his lord's commands; and the Marquis sought his wife to see how she would behave toward him. Both that day and ever afterward she was the same as at the time of their marriage, always pleasant and meek and loving and ready to serve him. Her grief she bore in silence, and never even spoke her daughter's name.

Four years later Griselda had another child, a boy; and now the whole country rejoiced that their ruler had a son to follow him. Alas, when it was two years old, the Marquis took a fancy to try his wife again. He said to her suddenly, "Wife, you know how displeased my people were at our marriage. Now that we have a son, they are more angry than ever. They say, 'When Walter is gone, the grandson of Janicula will be our ruler.' I cannot endure this murmuring; I want to live in peace with my people; and there is nothing else to do but to make way with the boy as I did with his sister. I tell you this beforehand so that you may not forget yourself when it comes to pass."

Griselda replied, "I have always said it was my pleasure to do your will. Even though you slay my daughter and my son, you have the right to do as you choose with your own; and if my own death would please you, I would gladly die."

The same officer with the hard, cruel face came to her and took her fair young son; and still she was so patient that she would not let her face look sad. She only kissed her boy and blessed him, and then, as before, she begged the man to bury the child where beasts and birds of prey would not find him; but he would give her no answer. This child, too, was carried to the sister of the Marquis at Bologna.

Marquis Walter watched his wife closely, but he could not see that she loved him less or was less eager to serve him and please him. It was quite different with his people, however, for the report had gone through the kingdom that the Marquis was no better than a murderer. For all that he would not give up his cruel purpose; and now he had planned even another test of his wife's faithfulness. He sent an envoy to Rome, bidding him on his return to bring back letters from the Pope to the effect that, as his marriage was making trouble and disorder in the kingdom, he should put away his wife and choose another bride, a lady of noble birth who would be better fitted to be his marchioness. The envoy obeyed his lord's commands and soon returned with letters all signed and sealed. Of course they were forged, but the simple folk of the country never thought of that. They were sad and grieved, and poor Griselda was saddest of all. Nevertheless, she kept her calmness and self-control and did not once forget her promise to her lord.

Griselda's daughter had been most tenderly cared for by the sister of the Marquis. For some years the Countess had been the wife of the Earl of Pavia, and to him the Marquis now sent a letter asking him to bring the two children to Saluces. They were to journey in all state and elegance, but no one was to be allowed to know who they were. "When people question," wrote the Marquis to his brother-in-law, "say to them that the maiden is on her way to wed the Marquis of Saluces."

All was done as the Marquis desired. The young maiden was dressed in the richest array and loaded with jewels for her marriage, and she and her brother set out in the care of the Earl to journey to Saluces, accompanied by a noble train of gentlefolk, all handsomely attired to do her honor.

The Marquis was bent upon trying his faithful wife to the uttermost, and one day in the presence of all the great folk of his court, he suddenly burst out rudely and said, "Griselda, when I married you, I did not look for wealth or noble birth, but for goodness and faithfulness and obedience. I realize now that if a man is a lord, he is also a servant of his people. A ploughman may take what wife he will, but matters are far different with a lord. My people are constantly urging me to choose a wife who is better fitted by rank and lineage for her position. The Pope understands the matter, and in order to quiet the disorders in my country, he has given his consent that I should take another bride. She is already on her way hither. Now do you be strong of heart and return to your father's house, leaving your place vacant for her. I will give you of my favor whatever dowry you brought with you. No one can always prosper, and I advise you to endure calmly whatever fortune decrees."

Griselda replied patiently, "My lord, I always knew that my poverty could not compare with your wealth; and I never thought myself worthy to be your wife or even your servant. I thank God that in my unworthiness you have honored me so long a while. I will return now to my father and stay with him in the little cottage where I was born until the day of my death shall come. God grant that with your new wife you may prosper and be happy. But, my dear lord, you know that when you took me from my father's house, you took no dowry with me, not even the poor clothes that I was wearing. Now here I give you back my wedding ring and these rich garments wherein it was your pleasure that I should dress. I ask you only for the undergarments which I wear, that I, who was once your wife, may not go forth in nakedness before the people."

"You may keep them," he answered coldly, and turned away. Then Griselda laid off her velvet and her pearls, and robed in white, her head and feet all bare, she went forth humbly to her father's house. The people followed her, sobbing and weeping in their grief, but not a tear did she shed. Her father tottered out from his poor cottage to meet his child, and threw his coat about her nakedness.

The Earl of Pavia had now arrived in the city from Bologna, and the news had gone abroad that he had brought with him a young maiden to become the Marquis's wife, and that she had come with such display of wealth as had never before been seen in Western Lombardy.

A messenger came in haste from the Marquis to his former wife, bidding her come straightway to the palace. Griselda obeyed, and humbly knelt before Lord Walter to hear his will. He said, "Griselda, tomorrow the maiden who is to become my wife comes to the palace, and I would wish her to be received with every possible honor. You know how I like my house to be, and I have sent for you that you may put every corner in such order as will please me."

"My lord," she replied, "the time will never come when I shall not love you with my whole heart and rejoice to serve you and please you so far as lies in my power." And without more words she set herself to work to arrange the house, to spread the tables, to make the beds, to hurry on the servants to sweep the floors and shake the rugs and hangings. She herself worked more diligently than all of them, and it was not long before hall and chambers were most perfectly arranged.

About nine in the morning the noble Earl arrived at the palace with the young maiden and her brother. Now folk are fickle and changeable as a weathercock, and in spite of all the love of Walter's people for Griselda, they were ready for something new. They even whispered among themselves that after all it was best that those who would wed should be of the same degree; and those who had had the good fortune to catch a glimpse of the face of the bride declared that she was verily even fairer than Griselda.

The wife whom the Marquis had cast away had gone to the gate with the other folk to greet the newcome Marchioness. She managed all things with such skill and cleverness that every guest was received according to his rank, and they wondered greatly who this could be that knew the custom of the house so well and yet was so meanly clad.

When the gentlefolk were about to seat themselves at the feast, the Marquis sent for Griselda to come to him. How do you like my fair young bride?" he questioned; and she answered, "I never saw a fairer maiden. God grant you prosperity and joy unto your life's end. But one wish I would make of you. This maid has been brought up more tenderly than I, and I pray and warn you not to wound her as you have wounded me, for she would hardly be able to endure adversity as one who has been less gently cared for."

Even this cruel Marquis could no longer bear to torture such a loving, faithful heart. He threw his arms about her neck, and kissed her again and again. "My Griselda," he said, "I have tested your steadfastness more severely than woman was ever tried before, and now shall come your reward. This fair maiden who you thought would be my bride is our beloved daughter. The manly boy beside her is our son, and he shall be my heir. I have kept them with my sister at Bologna, with charge to bring them up right carefully. I did not do this thing in malice, but to prove your faithfulness to me and to your promised word."

Griselda looked like one who had been startled out of her sleep. As she began to understand the Marquis's words, she swooned for joy; and then, arising from her swoon, she called her children to come to her. She put her arms about them and kissed them once and many a time, and dropped her tears upon their bright shining hair. She thought of nothing but the joy of seeing the dear ones whom she had supposed long since dead. "May God reward you, my dear lord," she cried, "that you have saved my children for me. It matters nothing if I should die this day, for now I know that my lord's love and favor are my own."

Those who stood about her wept great tears of pity, and the Marquis cheered and comforted his wife, and many looks of tenderest affection passed between them. As soon as the ladies saw their time, they led the Marchioness apart into a chamber, and there they stripped her of her rude gown and put upon her a robe of gleaming cloth of gold, and set upon her head a glittering crown that shone with many a jewel, and then they brought her back into the hall to take her proper place. So it was that this sad day came to a joyful ending; for every wedding guest did his utmost to make the feasting gay and to do her honor.

For many years the Marquis and his wife lived together in peace and joyfulness, and in the palace there was a place for the good Janicula, who dwelt there till his death. The fair young daughter was wedded to a rich and noble lord, one of the worthiest in all Italy. And when the time came for the Marquis to render up his soul to God who gave it him, his son succeeded to the heritage. He wedded a wife who loved him truly and was ever faithful to him; but he was wiser and more tender than his father, and never put her to such a sad and cruel test.

# X

# The Squire's Tale

## CAMBUSCAN AND THE BRAZEN HORSE

# The Squire's Tale

EVERYTHING had gone on well with the pilgrims. There had been little disagreement, and all had obeyed the host whom they had made their governor. It was now the morning of the fourth day, and good Harry Bailey rode nearer to the handsome young squire and said, "Squire, can't you tell us a good love story?" and he added slyly, "Surely, you must know as much about the matter as anyone."

"No, sir," the squire replied, "but I will do as well as I can. I will tell you a story, and if I do not tell it well, I can only ask your pardon. My will is good, at all events, and here is the tale."

## CAMBUSCAN AND THE BRAZEN HORSE

AT Sarray, in the land of Tartary, there once dwelt a king named Cambuscan. He was a noble, upright man, hardy and wise, and he was ever faithful to the religion to which he was born. He was a bold warrior, too. He had fought so fiercely against Russia that in his wars full many a brave man had come to his death. But in spite of all the fighting that had fallen to his lot, he was as eager to win glory in arms as any fresh-made knight of his house. He was handsome

101

and strong, and he lived in such royal state as one could hardly find anywhere else in the world.

This noble king was blessed with two sons, Algarsife and Camballo. He had also a daughter named Canacee; but there is no use in my trying to tell you how beautiful she was, for I have neither the words nor the skill to do such a thing; it would need a great rhetorician, and I am only a plain man. I must speak as I can.

Now when it came to the twenty-first year of the reign of Cambuscan, he sent out a proclamation through Sarray, as he was wont to do, that the thirteenth of March, his birthday, should be celebrated. When the day had come, the weather was bright and pleasant, the sun was joyous and clear, and the little birds sitting in its beams sang their merriest lays. They seemed to be rejoicing that they were no longer pierced by the cold, keen sword of winter.

There was to be a feast at the palace, and when the hour had come, Cambuscan put on his diadem and his richest robes and took his seat on the dais. Then came the feast; and I will tell you the truth, that never in all the world was there another feast so sumptuous. It would take the longest day in summer to describe half the courses and the order of service at each course. Then, too, there were all sorts of delicacies that are not known in this land. But no one can tell everything; I will go on and relate the tale.

Three courses were done, and the King sat among his nobles listening to the music of the minstrels, when suddenly through the door of the hall there came in a knight riding on a steed of brass. In his hand there was a broad glass mirror, on his thumb was a gold ring, and by his side hung a naked sword. The music stopped, not a word was spoken, and everyone gazed curiously at the strange knight. He was most richly armed save that he wore no helmet. He rode straight up to the table and made his obeisance to the King and Queen and lords in their order so reverently and gracefully that if Gawain with his oldtime courtesy had come forth from the realm of Faerie, he could have done no better. Then, standing before the high table, he gave his message in straightforward, manly fashion. As nearly as I can recall it, this is what he said:—

"My liege lord, King of Araby and of India, gives you greeting on this your festival day; and sends you by me, your servant, this steed of brass that in the space of a day can carry you through sunshine or shower to whatever place you may choose. If you should take a fancy to rise as high in the air as the eagle flies, this horse will bear you up, up, as high as ever you may wish to go; and he will move so gently that you can sleep on his back if you choose. When you are ready to descend, just twirl a certain wooden pin, and the horse will come down as softly as a feather. The workman who made the horse knew all about seals and magic bonds. Many a constellation he watched, waiting until the stars were favorable.

"The mirror that I hold in my hand is of such virtue that in it you may see when trouble is at hand, whether to you or to your kingdom. It will tell you who is a true friend and who is a secret foe. More than that, if a maiden love a man, she shall know by this glass whether he is true to her or not; and if he be false, there in the mirror will be the portrait of his new love. Nothing can be hidden. All his trickery will be open to her eyes. My king sends this mirror to the fair Lady Canacee, your excellent daughter.

"He sends her, too, this ring; and if it should chance that she would like to know the speech of birds and green things that grow, then let her wear this ring upon her thumb or carry it in her purse, and, truly, there is no bird flying under the heavens whose language she shall not understand; and she shall also be able to answer each one in its own tongue. And there shall not be a blade of grass growing out of the ground that shall not have a voice for her ears. She shall know, too, what virtue it hides within itself to heal the suffering or the wounded, and so shall she have power to cure him whom she will, however deep and wide his wounds may be.

"This naked sword that hangs close by my side has other virtue, but of no less worth. If with this sword in your hand you strike a blow, then shall it cut and pierce through all the armor of your foe, be it thick and firm as a branching oak. More than this, the wound shall never heal unless of your favor you may choose to stroke it with the flat of the sword. This is an amazing story, but it is the simple truth; and while the sword remains in your possession, its power shall never fail."

Again the knight bowed low before the King, then rode out of the hall into the court. The brazen horse flashed in the sunshine like a flame of fire, but stood as motionless as a stone. The knight was led to his room with all courtesy, unarmed, and brought in to the feast. The sword and the mirror were carried by some officers of rank to the tower, and with much ceremony the ring was presented to the Lady Canacee. As for the horse, there was no question what should be done with that, for, try as they might, all the servants of the King together could not stir it a hand's breadth. Neither windlass nor pulley would move it, for these men had no knowledge of the secret pin; therefore, they had good reason to leave it standing in the courtyard.

Of course the story spread like flame, and the people from all the country roundabout came in crowds to gaze at the marvelous horse. "See how tall and broad and long he is!" said some. "He has just the right shape and proportion to be strong. He must be of the Lombardy breed." But others said, "No; see how graceful he is and what a quick eye he has! That is more like a gentle Apulian courser." But of whatever blood they thought him, all agreed that certainly no horse that promised greater strength or speed or gentleness or endurance had ever been seen in the kingdom.

Of course the marvel was how a horse made of brass could move as this one had shown that it could. "It is a work of Faerie," the crowd declared. They shook their wise heads and fancied all sorts of explanations. They buzzed and murmured like a swarm of bees. They told over and over the fables and tales of old. One said it must be the winged horse Pegasus. Another insisted that it was the veritable steed of Sinon, the Greek who brought about the downfall of Troy, as the old histories say. "I believe some armed men are in that horse," declared one with a shudder, "and they will try to take the city; the King and his officers ought to know this and take good heed of it." Another whispered softly, "There's no truth in that. I believe this thing is only an apparition, like those that jugglers bring about by magic at great feasts." So they wondered and surmised, as ignorant people are wont to do when things are beyond their comprehension.

These simple folk had also much to say of the mirror that had been carried up into the highest tower. They wondered how people could see such things in it as the knight had said. One thought this might be brought about by an arrangement of angles and secret reflections, and recalled having heard that there was once such an one in Rome. Some spoke of Vitulan and Alacen and Aristotle, and said that in their books there were accounts of strange mirrors and perspective glasses. Others could talk of nothing but the sword that would cut through any kind of armor. They told tales of King

Telephus and of a certain magical spear that Achilles was said to have had which would both wound and heal. They talked about the effects of various drugs, about different ways of hardening metal, and of just when it should be done.

Then they had much to say about Canacee's ring. Some declared that they never before heard of such amazing skill in ring-making. Others recalled the story that both Moses and King Solomon were said to have had wonderful knowledge of how to make such things. Still others insisted that it was no more wonderful to make such a ring than it was to make glass out of fern ashes. "The only difference," they declared, "is that the ring is new to us and we have known about the glass for so long a while that people have stopped gabbling about it. Folk thought thunder and the ebb and flow of the tide and gossamer and mist, and, indeed, everything else, were most mysterious till they discovered the cause."

So they chattered and declared and fancied till the King rose from the table. The loud playing of the minstrels went before him till he came to his room where were his handsomest hangings and his richest ornaments. Then there was such music that one who heard it might well have deemed himself in heaven.

Now was the time for the merry dancing. The King seated himself upon his throne, and the stranger knight led out Canacee to the dance. No one but Launcelot could ever have described to you the many kinds of dances, the fresh, bright faces, the sly glances of jealousy. Launcelot is dead, so I must pass over all this merriment. I will say no more, but leave them to their pleasure till the hour for the supper had come.

The steward called for spices and wine, and all ate and drank. When they had had their fill, they went to the temple; and after the service was done, they sat down to supper, while it was yet daylight. Why should I describe the many viands at the supper? Everyone knows that when a king gives a feast, there are all sorts of dainties, and that the humblest as well as he who is most worthy of respect has plenty of each.

After supper the noble King went to examine the brazen steed, and a great company of lords and ladies went with him. Surely, there was never so much wondering about a horse before since the days of the horse of Troy. They talked and they looked and they marveled;

and then the King asked the knight to tell him how to manage the steed. The knight replied, "Sir, there is really nothing more to learn. When you wish to go anywhere, twirl the pin in his ear—I will tell you about this privately—and tell him the name of the place to which you wish to go. That is all there is to it. And when you have come to where you would stop, twirl another pin and tell him to descend, and he will go down at once. Moreover, he will stand precisely where you leave him; and even if the whole world should try to move him, they would not be able to stir him from the place. If you wish to send him away from you, twirl this other pin, and he will vanish from sight. When you want him again, you have only to call him in a way that I will teach you when we are by ourselves. So are you free to ride wherever you wish."

This brave and noble King soon learned from the knight the secret of the pins. He had the bridle carried to the tower to be kept among his most precious jewels; and he bade the horse disappear. Then, glad of heart at possessing such a treasure, he returned to the revelings. All night long, and almost to the coming of the day, Cambuscan and his lords feasted in merriment and jollity.

As the dawning drew near, one after another grew sleepy, and at last all the King's visitors had gone to their beds. They slept till it was broad daylight. Canacee, however, was more moderate. She had gone to her rest soon after the evening had begun, for she had no idea of looking pale in the morning. After her first sleep she awoke, and she felt so delighted with her curious ring and her mirror that her color came and went, not once but twenty times. She went to sleep again, but even in her sleep she had a vision of the mirror. She was wide awake before sunrise, and she called her governess, who slept close by, and said she wished to rise. The governess said, "Madame, folk are all at rest. Where will you go so early?" "I will get up and walk out a little," Canacee replied. So the governess called ten or twelve of the ladies in waiting. Canacee was soon ready, and was as fresh and bright as the sun himself. She dressed herself in light clothes, for it was a mild and pleasant season, and roamed about in the park with only five or six of her attendants. The mist rising from the south made the sun look broad and red. It was the beautiful morning time; birds were singing, and the hearts of all the company leaped up with joy; but Canacee had still more reason to rejoice, for she found that she could understand the meaning of every song.

Now high above the head of the princess, in an old tree dry and white as chalk, sat a falcon. She was wondrously beautiful, so fair both in color and in form that she looked like a wanderer from some strange and marvelous country. She seemed to be in sore distress; for she cried so piteously that the whole wood echoed, and she had beaten her wings so harshly that the red blood was running down the tree. And she never ceased crying and shrieking and plucking the feathers from her breast so cruelly that there is not a tiger or any other beast that would not have wept—if he could weep—for pity of her.

Canacee still had on her finger the ring that the knight had brought, and so of course she could understand everything that the bird said and could answer it again. For some time she stood watching, then she said, "Will you not tell me why it is that you are in such anguish? It must be because someone dear to you has died, or else that someone has been false to you in love. Tell me your trouble, I beg. I am a king's daughter, and if you will only come down from the tree, I will do all in my power to remove your sorrow; and, too, I know the use of many an herb, and I can easily find some to cure your wounds."

The falcon made no reply save to cry more piteously than before. Then she fell to the ground and lay there in a swoon. Canacee took her up and held her tenderly till she had come to herself. She told a sad tale of a tercelet that had won her heart, and then deserted her for love of a fair young kite; and as she spoke, the tears of Canacee fell like rain, and all her women shared in her sorrow. How to comfort the hawk was the question. Canacee wrapped her softly in bandages, dug herbs, and made salves to heal her. She carried her most gently to the palace, and she worked from morning till night, trying to help her. Close to the head of her bed she made a cage and covered it with velvet of blue, the color of truth, in token of the truth that is in woman.[1]

[Now, sirs, I fear much that you will blame me sorely for an unfinished tale, but I can only do my best. I would gladly rehearse to you a lengthy account of the conquests of this great King Cambuscan, of how many cities he won; also of Algarsife and Camballo, how they

---

[1]Chaucer did not complete this story. The ending given here was written by Edmund Spenser nearly two hundred years later. See the *Faerie Queen,* book iv, cantos 2 and 3.

107

were wondrously aided in their exploits by the magic steed of brass; but, truly, sirs, he from whom I had the tale could tell me nothing of its ending. When I bewailed this to a learned friend who dwelt here in our own country, he of his courtesy most kindly offered to partly end the tale, for either had he heard some distant legend, or else to his own mind—for verily, sirs, he was a poet—had come the fancy, and he knew not whence. This is the ending that he gave.]

Fair Canacee was truly loved by many a lord and many a knight of greatest worthiness; but she refused to give herself to either knight or lord of high degree. Therefore it came to pass that quarrels rose among her lovers, and often they fought most grievously. Camballo, her wise brother, saw that this would lead to battles and, it might be, to rending of the kingdom. One day when many of her lovers, warlike men and bold, had met together, and there seemed like to be a bloody slaughter for her sweet sake, Camballo bade them listen to his words.

"That all this strife may cease," he said, "I here proclaim a trial by arms, and Lady Canacee shall be its prize. Do all you who would win my sister's hand choose from among you three, the stoutest and the bravest of the company. With those three, each one in turn, will I hold combat; and he who overcomes the brother shall win the sister for his wife."

Then there was silence among the suitors, and one by one they drew back from the challenge. They were brave young men, these knights and lords; but it was known among them that Camballo had a magic ring of such virtue that no matter how often or how severely he was wounded, the wound would close at once and heal. "We fight with mortals, not with Faerie," said the knights; and finally none were left to seek the prize save three brave brothers of such valor that they would give up their lives rather than withdraw.

The day for the contest arrived. The lists were made ready; six judges were chosen to view the deeds of arms; and on a lofty platform fair Canacee was set to be the prize of him who should win her by his bravery. The knights advanced in shining armor. Camballo entered first alone into the lists with stately steps and fearless countenance. To meet him came the three brothers with gilded scutcheons and broad banners widely floating. They made humble obeisance to fair Canacee; the trumpets and the clarions sounded loud and shrill, and such a fight began as men have rarely witnessed.

To make a long story short, I will say that, brave as were the brothers and furious as were their cuts and thrusts, they had small chance in contest with a foe whose every wound was healed almost as soon as given; and the first two were slain before much time had passed. The fight with the third, however, was as fierce as if Camballo was contending with three rather than one; and, indeed, he was, though he knew it not. The mother of these three brothers was a fay who knew all secret things. She discovered by her magic arts that the lives of her sons would be short, and she besought the Fates to bestow upon her a single boon. "When the first shall die," she pleaded, "grant that all remaining of the space of his life's natural term shall be given to the second; and that when he, too, shall come to his death, all that remains of his life and strength and that of his brother shall be added to the third." This prayer was granted, and this is why the contest waxed so fierce, for Camballo was not fighting with one, however stout and hardy he might be, but with three doughty champions.

Suddenly a loud clamor was heard, and a strange chariot, decked with gold and gorgeous ornaments and drawn by two savage lions, dashed through the crowd and into the lists like a whirlwind. A lady of rarest beauty sat in the chariot. In her right hand she bore a rod of peace, and in her left was a magic potion called nepenthe. She greeted first her brother, and then Camballo; though to Camballo she spoke but shyly, for at the first glance at him she felt young love arising in her heart. They paid her small attention, and even her prayers and tears that they would cease their strife availed her not at all. Then with the magic power that she had learned from her mother, wise in Faerie lore, she stood upright and touched them lightly with her wand of peace. Their swords dropped from their hands, and they stood staring at each other in amazement. "Drink," bade the maiden; and she held out to them her golden cup, filled with the drink that brings forgetfulness. As soon as they had drunk from this, their contest was forgotten. Each saw in the man before him so brave and noble a champion that he had no choice but to love him and respect him. So it was that each one gave a friendly kiss unto the other. They clasped each other's hand and pledged their word that ever after this they would be true and faithful friends, and stand by each other in both woe and weal.

The people shouted in wonder and in joy till the very heavens rang. Canacee descended from her lofty seat and gave warm greeting to the stranger. Then in the gorgeous chariot, sitting side by side, the two fair maidens rode homeward as if dear and loving sisters.

So it was that gentle Canacee was won; and, to make the tale some few words longer, so it was that Camballo gained a wife with whom he passed long years of happiness.

# XI

# The Franklin's Tale

## THE PROMISE OF DORIGEN

# The Franklin's Tale

IN faith, young squire," said the franklin heartily, "you have done well. According to my judgment there is not one here who is your equal in eloquence."

"Come, Mr. Franklin," the host broke in, "you know that each of you must tell at least one or two tales or break his word."

"That know I, sir," responded the franklin, "but I beg you do not hold me faithless if I speak a word or two to this man."

"But first tell us your tale," cried Harry Bailey.

"I obey your will," replied the franklin courteously. "Here is my story. If I can only tell it in such wise as to please you, then I shall know that it is well done."

## THE PROMISE OF DORIGEN

THERE was once in the land of Brittany a knight named Arviragus, who was doing his best to win the love of a noble lady, the fairest under the sun. He carried on many a bold enterprise and undertook many a perilous adventure all for her sake, that she might perchance look with the more favor upon his suit. She came of such high lineage that he hardly dared to tell her of his devotion; but when he did confess it, he found that he had already won his bride, for he was so sincere and humble and in every way worthy that she could not help loving him, and she promised to take him for her husband and her lord. He, too, made a promise, and vowed to her most solemnly that, come what would, he would never force her obedience against her wish, nor would he show jealousy of her, but would obey her and follow her will in everything, as a true lover should ever do to his lady. "And I give you here my troth," said Dorigen, for that was her name, "that until my last day I will be your faithful, humble wife."

The couple dwelt in happiness for a year and more. Then they were separated, for the knight went to England for a year or two to seek for glory in arms. Dorigen could hardly endure his absence. She wept and she sighed, she moaned and wailed and so longed for Arviragus that the whole wide world seemed nothing to her without him. Her castle stood near the sea, and she used often to go to the edge of the cliff and watch the ships and barges; but this gave her small comfort, for she said to herself, "Alas, there are so many ships sailing freely wherever they will, and not one of them brings my dear lord home to me. If he would only come, my heart would be eased of this bitter pain."

Sometimes she would not watch the ships, but would only sit on the cliff and muse and think of her husband. Then if it happened that her glance fell upon the black, jagged rocks below her, she would tremble so that she could not stand upon her feet; for she would fancy that each one was threatening to destroy the vessel that was to bring him home, when the happy day of his return should arrive.

Her friends tried in every way they knew to comfort her. They often visited her, they told her that Arviragus would surely return, that she was destroying herself for nothing; and then they would beg her to come out with them. At first they walked by the ocean, but they soon saw that the sight of the water dashing against the black ledges only made her the more wretched. "I wish to God that all those fearful black rocks were sunk into hell for the sweet sake of my lord. They make my very heart quake with fear," she exclaimed. The friends did not ask her again to walk with them by the shore. Instead of that, they persuaded her to go by springs and along the riverbank and to other beautiful places. They prevailed upon her to play at chess and tables and to dance. One bright morning in May they induced her to go with them to a beautiful garden where they meant to spend the entire day.

This garden was a charming place. The gentle showers of May had filled it full of leaves and blossoms, and the hand of man had given it such wise and skillful care that save, it may be, for Paradise, there was never so lovely a place. The sweetness of the flowers and the sight of their freshness and beauty would make the heart of anyone light, unless it was burdened with so deep woe that nothing could give it cheer.

These friends of Dorigen had brought dainty viands with them that they might remain the whole of the day; and after they had dined, they began to sing and to dance on the soft green turf. Even the sight of the dancing made Dorigen grieve, because her husband was not among the merry revelers. Nevertheless, she would not be so rude as to break away from her kind friends, so she waited sad and lonely in her heart.

As she sat, gazing listlessly at the dancers, there was a certain young squire who was gazing at her, but by no means listlessly. He was fresher and more gayly clad than the month of May itself. He sang more sweetly and he danced more gracefully than anyone else, and he certainly was one of the handsomest young men in the world. He was young and strong and rich, highly esteemed, and a favorite wherever he went; and, to make a long story short, for two years this young squire Aurelius had loved Dorigen better than all the world beside. He had never dared to tell her his love, but he composed many songs, rounds, and virelays about the agonies of one who adores and is not loved in return. In his songs he said that, like Echo, who died for the love of Narcissus, so he should die for her who was so dear to him; and she would never know why he had come to an early death. Writing these songs was his greatest pleasure; but Dorigen never guessed that he was writing them of her, and when in the dances of the young folk he had gazed piteously into her face like one beseeching some great favor, she had not understood that he was silently begging her to receive his devotion. As they had long been acquaintances, it was natural that they should meet and talk together for a while. "Madam," said he, "if it would please you, I could find it in my heart to wish that on the day when your Arviragus crossed the sea, I, too, had gone somewhere never to return; for I know well that my devotion to you will have for its reward only the breaking of my heart. Pity me, Madam, pity me, for I am so unhappy that I would I lay in a grave at your feet. Have mercy upon me, or you will be my death; for to think that you will never be mine is more than I can bear."

Dorigen started and looked him full in the face. "I call my God to witness," she said gravely, "that Arviragus is my true and beloved husband, and never shall I leave him for any other;" and she added solemnly, "Go and gaze upon those black and jagged rocks that have sent so many a good ship to her destruction and that threaten the safety of my dear husband, and know that when every one of those rocks has vanished, I will leave my Arviragus for you, and never before. Thrust this folly from your heart. What pleasure can it be to a man to love another man's wife?"

Then appeared Dorigen's friends who had been roaming about in the garden and had no idea what had been going on between her and Aurelius. The dancing and gayety lasted till the bright sun had gone below the horizon. Then they all went home merrily save Aurelius. When he had reached his home, he dropped upon his knees, and in the agony of his heart he called upon Phœbus Apollo to come to his aid and work a miracle for him that he might so win his lady.

"Gracious Apollo, god of the sun," he prayed, "help me, I beg. Grant that you will beseech your radiant sister Lucina, goddess of the moon, that she will bring so high a tide that it will flow over the loftiest rock on the coast of Brittany. Beg her, I entreat you, to go no faster than you in her course, then shall she be ever at the full, and there shall be high tide both night and day. If she refuses this prayer, then I beseech you to sink the rocks down to the realm of darkness where Lord Pluto dwells. Pity my pain, Lord Phœbus. Help me, and I will make barefoot pilgrimage to your temple at Delphos."

Time passed, and Arviragus came home with wealth and honors, and joyfully betook himself to his Dorigen. No words can express her gladness at having again her dearly beloved husband; and as for him, he felt more and more happy every day in the love of so devoted a wife.

As for Aurelius, Lord Phœbus had not answered his prayer, and he lay in suffering and longing for Dorigen all this while. No one knew of his pain except his brother. This brother wept and grieved with him, and lay awake night after night, trying to think of some way to help the luckless lover to win the lady. Suddenly the thought of an old book that he had seen at Orleans in France when a student came into his mind. It was a book of magic; and it told of marvelous deeds that had been done, or that appeared to those looking on to have been done. His heart danced for joy, for he said to himself, "I do believe that there is a way for my brother to be cured. I have often heard that jugglers, coming into a hall of feasting, could make the feasters think that they saw within the hall a lake, and in the lake a barge floating up and down; or that they beheld a savage lion springing in at the door, or flowers growing up as if in a meadow, or a vine producing red and white grapes, or even a castle built of solid lime and stone." He told all this to his brother, and then he said, "Now if I can find at Orleans some one of my old companions who knows magic, surely he can help us. It cannot be so very difficult to make it appear for a day or two as if there were no rocks on the coast of Brittany, and as if ships were sailing up to the very shore."

Aurelius felt as hopeful as his brother. He started up from his bed, and the two set off for Orleans. When they were but two or three furlongs from the city, they met a young scholar walking alone who greeted them in Latin. Then he said, "I know why you have come to Orleans;" and he went on to tell them the whole story of Aurelius's sufferings and their hope that in Orleans they might find help. It was plain that he was a magician, and when he invited them to his house, they went with him most gladly.

At the magician's home there was much to see. Their host showed them parks full of wild deer, larger than any that the brothers had ever seen before. Then he let them watch a deer hunt, and with their own eyes they saw deer wounded and a hundred slain. Then they saw a beautiful winding river whereon were falconers with their hawks taking heron. And after this they saw a tournament, knights jousting on a plain. After the tournament came a dance, and behold, one of the dancers was Dorigen. Aurelius was more than an onlooker here, for he, too, seemed to be joining the revelry. Oh, it was a marvelously delightful entertainment; but suddenly the magician clapped his hands. All the wonderful sights vanished. There in the quiet library sat the host and his two guests, and there they had been from the time that they entered the house; for all these wonderful sights had been brought before them by the power of magic.

The master called his squire and said, "It is now nearly an hour since I and my two guests came into my library. Is the supper ready?"

117

"Sir," replied the squire, "the table stands waiting, for all things are prepared."

"Then we will go and sup," said the master. "Even these eager lovers have to eat and rest."

There was no question that this was a magician of amazing power. After what the brothers had seen, they did not doubt that he could do so small a thing as conceal a few rocks from view for a while; and so, when their supper had been eaten, they fell to business. There was no need of explanations or long stories to a man so wise that he knew them all beforehand; so they asked him directly what guerdon he would demand for removing every rock on the coast of Brittany from the Gironde to the mouth of the Seine.

"That is not so easy a task," the magician declared. "It is quite a different matter from sitting quietly in a library and showing you a few deer and a little jousting. I would not attempt it for any trifling reward. I could not think of undertaking it for less than a thousand pounds; and verily, I am not eager to do it at any price."

"A thousand pounds!" Aurelius cried joyfully, "that is nothing. Folk say the world is round, and I would gladly give the whole round world if I were lord of it. I take your offer, master; the bargain is made. You shall have your payment on the instant; but do not delay us here one moment beyond tomorrow morning."

"I pledge my faith to you," responded the magician.

As soon as the morrow had come, they went to Brittany by the nearest way. The master set to work at once with his spells and magic circles and incantations; but, work as fast as ever he could, he could not satisfy the restless Aurelius, who would one moment bow in reverence to his knowledge and the next moment threaten to run him through with his sword because he worked so slowly. At length, however, the marvel was accomplished, not a rock was to be seen. Aurelius fell down at the master's feet and thanked him, and begged his pardon most humbly if in his eagerness he had done aught amiss.

He went straight to Dorigen, fell on his knees before her, and said, "Madam, do you remember that of your great kindness you promised that when every rock on the coast should have disappeared, you would leave Arviragus and come to me as my wife? Behold, Madam, not one remains in sight;" and then he took his leave.

Dorigen stood like a statue, her face as white as marble; for it had never entered her mind that such a miracle could come to pass. She gazed out upon the water, where not one rock was visible; she gazed shudderingly down the path taken by Aurelius; and then she went to her own house; but not to rest, for there she wept and wailed and groaned and swooned. She had no comfort in her woe and no one to whom she might venture to tell her trouble, for Arviragus was from home.

When her husband returned, he asked her why she wept; and at this she only wept the more. "Oh, that I had never been born!" she groaned. Arviragus did his best to soothe and comfort her, and at length she told him the sad story, how fearful she had been lest the boat which bore her love might come to grief on the sharp-pointed rocks, and how, wearied and indignant at the persistency of Aurelius, she had declared, half in grave anger and half in scorn, "Yes, when those black, threatening rocks on Brittany's coast have disappeared, then will I leave my dear Arviragus and come to you."

Her husband comforted her as well as he could, for his own heart was breaking. When she was somewhat soothed, he said quietly, but in the deepest sorrow, "My Dorigen, truth is the noblest thing in the world. I love you so that I would rather lose you and have you true than keep you with a broken promise." The strong man burst into a flood of tears; but as soon as he could speak, he bade her leave him and go to find Aurelius, "and I will bear my woe as best I can," he said.

Then Dorigen went forth from her husband's house almost mad with grief. Aurelius in the hope of seeing her had hardly taken his eyes from her door, and now he walked by a way where they could not help meeting. As soon as he saw her, he saluted her with a most eager curtsy; but she only moaned, "Alas, alas!" and he entreated her to tell him what her grief might be. When the story came to his ears, then, anxious as he was to win her, yet he could not help pitying her and honoring that noble man, her husband, who loved his wife so dearly and so unselfishly that he would rather lose her than have her break her word.

Then said Aurelius, "Madam, farewell. You are the best and truest wife that I have ever seen in all this land. Perchance a squire can do a courtesy as well as a knight. So go you back to your dear lord Arviragus, and say to him that, as he would rather have you keep your promise and leave him to suffer, so should I rather suffer all my life with longing for you than come between you and your love; and so I bid you my farewell."

119

She knelt before him, and thanked him; and then she went home to her sorrowing husband and told him all. And from that day their lives passed on in happiness and peace; for never was there shadow of disagreement between them, and day by day they loved each other more dearly.

There is but one more word to say, and that concerns the thousand pounds. "Alas," groaned Aurelius, "that I have promised a thousand pounds of gold to this magician. What shall I do? I could pay him a portion every year and thank him for his great courtesy, if he will permit; but if I have to pay him all at once, I must sell my lands and live a beggar; there is no other way. Whatever comes, I will not lie; I will keep my promised word."

With a sad heart he went to his treasury and took out five hundred pounds. Then he went to the magician and said, "Master, I have never yet broken my word, and my debt to you shall be paid if I have to go forth from my home as a beggar; but if I give you surety, would you grant me a delay of two or three years? If not, I must sell my lands."

The magician demanded sternly, "Did I not keep my agreement with you?"

"Surely you did, and to the letter," the squire replied.

"Did you not win your lady?" the magician asked.

"Oh no," said the squire, and sighed sorrowfully.

"How was that? I pray you tell me if you can."

Aurelius told the whole story, and ended with the words, "Arviragus would rather die in sorrow than that his wife should be false to her word; so he bade her come to me. Dorigen had never heard of magical appearances when she gave her promise, and she sorrowed so sadly that I sent her back to him. That is all; there is no more to the story."

The magician answered, "Dear brother, he is a knight and you are a squire, but you were equally noble. Now surely a clerk can do as honest a deed as any of you; and, therefore, sir, I release you from the thousand pounds as freely as if I had never seen you. You paid well for my food and lodging, and not a penny will I take for either skill or work. It is enough. Farewell, and good-day."

Now of these three generous men, which one was the most generous?

# XII

## The Canon's Yeoman's Tale

### THE PRIEST WHO LEARNED TO BE
### A PHILOSOPHER

# The Canon's Yeoman's Tale

WHILE the pilgrims were riding onward at a good pace, two men were galloping after them at full speed. They proved to be a canon and his servant, or yeoman, and they had been doing their best to catch up with the company. The yeoman was especially ready to talk, and before long he had explained that his lord was a great alchemist. "He could even pave with gold and silver all this ground over which we have been riding," he declared.

"Why, then, does he wear clothes so torn and soiled?" asked the host, "if he can make gold so easily?"

"The trouble is," replied the yeoman, "that he is overwise; and when a man has too great a wit, it often happens that he fails to use it aright." Then the talkative yeoman went on to explain that his master was wont to borrow gold by making the lenders believe that he could multiply it twentyfold. "We always hope that we can do this," declared the yeoman; "but knowledge is so far ahead of us that we never seem to overtake it; and I fear it will make beggars of us at last."

The canon began to suspect that his man was telling too many tales. He went nearer to him and whispered angrily, "Hold your peace. If you talk any more, you shall be sorry for it. You are slandering me here in this company and telling what you should be wise enough to hide."

"Tell on," cried the host, who had overheard the threat, "no matter what comes. Don't trouble yourself about his threatening."

"In faith, no more I do," declared the yeoman; and when the canon alchemist found that his secrets were to be revealed, he galloped away as fast as his horse would carry him.

The yeoman told more of the craft of the canon, his master, and then he began his tale.

# THE PRIEST WHO LEARNED TO BE A PHILOSOPHER

THERE was once in London a priest who had no church, but spent his time in singing masses for the dead. He boarded with a good dame of the town, and in the house he was so pleasant and helpful to her that she would not allow him to pay her for either his food or his clothes. His expenses, then, were so small that he always had a goodly supply of money on hand.

Now one day a false canon came to him and begged him for a loan for three days. "If you will lend me a mark," he said, "I will pay it on the moment. Hang me by the neck if I break my word." The priest gave him the mark. The canon thanked him over and over, and said farewell. He kept his promise to the letter, and brought the priest his money the moment it was due.

The good priest was much pleased. "It is certainly a pleasure," he said, "to lend a man a noble, or two or three, or anything else that I possess, for that matter, when he keeps his word so well, and returns the loan on the instant. I could never say no to such a man."

"I hope you did not think for a moment that I could be false!" exclaimed the canon. "That would, indeed, be something new. God forbid that from now to my life's end I should fail to keep my word. You may believe that as firmly as you believe your creed. I thank God that never yet have I failed to pay every grain of gold or silver that was ever lent me, that never yet have I even thought falsehood in my heart. And now, sir," he continued, "since you have been so kind and courteous to me, I should like to return the favor. I will tell you what I will do. I will show you the whole secret of how I work in philosophy. Only watch, and before I go you shall see with your own eyes a real masterpiece. But perhaps you do not care for philosophy?"

"Not care for philosophy?" repeated the priest; "I beg you with all my heart to show me the kindness."

"Surely, sir, if you wish it," said the canon; and he began his preparations on the instant. "Will you order your yeoman to go and buy us two or three ounces of quicksilver; and when he returns with it, I will show you a greater wonder than you ever saw before in all your life."

The priest was only too ready to consent. "Go as fast as ever you can," he bade his yeoman, "and fetch us three ounces of quicksilver."

In a very short time the yeoman was back again with the quicksilver. The canon took it, and told the yeoman to bring some hot coals. The coals were brought. Then the canon drew from under his robe a crucible. The priest was watching each motion, for it is not every man who has a chance to learn the secret of a philosopher.

The canon held up the crucible and gazed at it a moment as if it was a most precious article. Then he held it toward the priest. "This is a crucible," he explained. "You may take it into your own hands and put into it one ounce of this quicksilver. That is the first step in the work of a philosopher. I tell you frankly there are not many men to whom I would reveal even so much of my secret. You shall see right here before your own face that I will destroy this quicksilver, and turn it into as pure, fine silver as there is in your purse or anywhere else for that matter, and I will make it malleable. If I do not, call me a liar if you will and not fit to live among honest folk. I have a powder for which I paid an enormous price, and in this is the secret of the whole matter. But send your yeoman away, I beg, for there must be no one to watch us while we are working in philosophy."

The priest was ready to do whatever the canon commanded. He told his servant to go, and he shut the door after him so closely that no one could possibly peep in; and then they went to work in earnest. "I shall treat you as a dear friend," declared the canon, "and so I am going to let you do everything yourself. Then you will fully learn the work and understand it, for you will have done it all with your own hands." So under his directions the priest set the crucible upon the coals and blew the fire. The canon cast into the crucible a powder, perhaps made of chalk, perhaps of glass, at any rate not worth a fly. "Blow up the coals," he cried, "and heap them up high above the crucible."

The priest obeyed every order with delight, for was he not learning to be a philosopher? But while he was blowing the fire and heaping up the coals, the rascally canon seized the opportunity to get a beechen coal of his own out from his bosom. This was no common coal, but one that the treacherous canon had prepared. He had carefully bored a hole in it, and filled it with an ounce of silver filings. Then he had stopped up the hole with wax. This coal he kept hidden in his hand. When the priest had heaped up the coal over the crucible, the canon looked at it somewhat doubtfully. Then he said, "Your pardon, friend, but that is not laid quite as it should be. Let me meddle with your work for but a moment and I will build it up for you. But how hard you are working! You are heated almost as hot as the crucible, and how you sweat! Here, take this cloth and wipe your face."

The priest took the cloth and wiped his face, and at the instant when his eyes were covered, what did that wicked canon do but crowd the coals together around the crucible, and directly over the middle of it he laid his beechen coal. Then he took the bellows and blew with all his might till the fire was all aglow.

Now I am thirsty," said the canon. "Let us have a drink. Everything is right and will come out well, I promise you. Let us sit down and make ourselves merry." So they sat down, and while they rested and drank, the fire burned, and before long the canon's beechen coal had burned also, and of course all the silver filings had melted and dropped down into the crucible. The simple priest knew nothing of the trick; he supposed all the coals were alike.

When the canon was sure that the silver was in the crucible, he said to the priest, "Rise up, sir priest. Come and stand beside me. I suppose that of course you have no mold, have you? Then will you go and bring a chalk stone, and I can perhaps shape that like a mold. Oh yes, and bring with you also a bowl or a pan of water; and then you shall see how our business gets on. Stop a moment. After I am gone, I don't want you to fancy that some trick was played you while you were out of the room, and so I will go with you and come back when you return." They opened the door and passed through it. Then they shut it, and locked it behind them, and went their way, carrying the key with them.

But there is no need of making so long a story of it. When they had brought back the chalk, the canon made it into the shape of a mold. He took out of his sleeve a thin plate of silver which weighed exactly one ounce, and he shaped his mold just as long and as wide as this. He made it so quickly and so slyly that the priest had not a suspicion of what he was doing. He hid the silver plate in his sleeve again and said cheerfully, "Now watch closely, for we shall surely succeed." He poured out the melted matter from the crucible into the mold and cast it into the vessel of water. Then he said to the priest, "Put your hand in and feel around. I certainly hope you will find silver." What else could it be, indeed? Silver shavings are silver, in faith.

The priest put his hand into the water and felt around, and in a minute he brought up a plate of fine silver. Then he was certainly the happiest priest in all London town. "The blessings of all the saints be upon you, sir canon," he exclaimed joyfully, "and their curse light upon me if I do not obey you in everything, provided you will vouchsafe to teach me this noble craft."

The canon nodded his assent, and then said thoughtfully, "It would be better to do this once more, so that you may have a chance to watch even more closely and become expert; and then when I am not here you can try it by yourself. Let us take another ounce of quicksilver and do with it precisely what we did with the first."

The priest needed no urging. He hurried as fast as ever he could to do as the canon commanded, and blew the fire with all his might and main. He no more dreamed that the canon had a second trick than that he had already played one. This time the canon held a hollow stick in his hand, in the end of which was one ounce of silver filings kept in by wax just as the filings were before kept in the coal. While the priest was busy obeying the master's orders, the canon cast more of the powder into the crucible, and with that cheat of a stick he stirred the heaped up coals until the wax had melted and every bit of the silver that was in the stick had fallen into the crucible.

Now this innocent priest was so pleased that he could not express his joy. "I will do anything for you," he said. "I give myself to you, body and goods."

Then said the canon, "I am only a poor man, but I promise you shall find me skillful. I warn you, however, that this is not all; there is yet more to be seen. Is there any copper in the house?"

"Yes, sir," the priest replied, "I believe there is."

"If not, go and buy us some as soon as may be, dear sir; hasten, I pray."

The priest went his way, and soon returned with the copper. The canon took it and weighed out just one ounce. He put this copper into the crucible, set the crucible on the fire, cast his powder into it, and told the priest to blow the coals, and to stoop down low, just as he did before. And this whole thing was nothing but a rascally trick! Afterwards he cast the mixture into the mold and put it into the water. This time he put in his own hand. In his sleeve he had a silver plate, as I have said. The wretch slyly took it out from his sleeve, the priest never dreaming of such cheating, and dropped it down to the bottom of the dish. Then he fumbled around in the water and very secretly slipped out the copper plate and hid it. After this he caught the simple priest by his gown and said merrily, "Stoop down and help me as I helped you a while ago. Put your hand in and see what you can find."

The priest took out the silver plate, and turned it over and over in his hand, and gazed upon it. The canon said, "Let us go now and carry these plates that we have been making to some goldsmith, and find out whether they are really good. I will wager my hood that they are good pure silver, and we will soon prove it."

They went to the goldsmith, and he tested the plates with fire and hammer, and declared that they were pure silver.

Poor, foolish priest, who was happier than he? There never was a bird more eager to greet the daylight or a nightingale more blithe in singing in the month of May, there never was a lady more joyful in caroling or in speaking of love and womanhood, there never was a knight more earnest to do some deed of hardihood that he might stand high in the grace of his lady, than was the priest to learn this wonderful art, and he begged of the canon, "For the love of God, and for the sake of whatever I may have deserved of you, what does this recipe cost? Tell me, I pray."

"In faith," the canon replied, "it is dear. In all England there is no one save myself and a friar who know it."

"No matter," cried the priest, "only tell me what I must pay. Tell me, I beg of you."

The shameless canon hesitated. At length he said, "Indeed, it is very costly, as I told you. Still, you have been most friendly to me.

You may have it for forty pounds; but it would cost a good deal more to anyone but you."

The priest was so afraid the canon would change his mind and refuse to give him the recipe after all that he brought out the forty pounds as quick as ever he could, and gave the money to the canon for his worthless recipe.

The canon put the money away carefully; then he said, "Sir priest, I have a favor to ask of you. If people knew what skill I have, they would be so envious of me that they would soon take my life. So if you love me, I pray you keep my secret."

"Never will I give word or hint of it to any living being," answered the priest earnestly. "I would rather give every penny I own than to have you fall into such trouble."

"I thank you kindly, sir priest," said the canon. "May you have good luck in return for your goodwill. Now fare you well." And so the canon went his way, and the priest never set eyes upon him again. Before long he made trial of the magical recipe; but, alas, this time there was no silver in the crucible.

Made in the USA
Monee, IL
16 August 2023

41120367R00077